Bone Orchard Gospel

Western role-playing in another world

This is not Earth.

Many of the conventions of Earth are the same, and players should expect nothing as wild or fantastic as wizard kings, dragon hordes, or lazerguns, but it still remains separate.

The world is known as Ludt.

The time is comparable to that of Earth's 1860s-1880s, specifically in the American West.

You are encouraged to be as 'Old West' as you want.

The Instigation

As a child I devoured western films avariciously, primarily those featuring the swaggering John Wayne. As I grew older I drifted away from westerns, but never lost interest in the romance of the setting. I will still gladly sit down to a Clint Eastwood film and thoroughly enjoyed the Coen Brothers' True Grit and Tarantino's entries into the genre. The structure of westerns has influenced many other genres which I hold dear as well, primarily science fiction and the original series of Star Trek, Firefly, and Westworld are three such series which either in content or structure mimic elements of the western genre. I have never read a western novel (other than Stephen King's Dark Tower, though that was after I had already begun this project), yet my players tell me that this game feels like a Louis Lamour novel. But I am a great fan of older country music, bluegrass, dark country, and neo-folk, all of which have served as great inspiration for me in this endeavor, as well as the wealth of historical information and creative art concerning the Old West, both as it existed and as it lives on in the communal imagination.

I do not remember my original inspiration for this game, only that I began it in 2012 or 2013 while living in a low-rent apartment at the edge of the world and studying film. Since that time it has served as a consistent source of entertainment for myself and any and all who have passed through the proverbial batwing doors of its entrance. With Bone Orchard Gospel (or B.O.G. as it is hereafter referred to) it is possible in a matter of minutes to throw yourself and your friends into a vivid and approachable mirror of a brutal and poetic sundown world where frontier justice is the law and a man is only as good as his gun. After almost a decade of keeping this project to myself I decided that it was high time I shared it with the rest of you.

B.O.G. is a role-playing game (or RPG), which is a type of game in which the players work together to create an exciting and original story together. One player will be the Judge, and will be in charge of telling the story, keeping it moving, and making decisions for the various events, villains, allies, and innocents in the tale; The second half of this book includes some simple guidelines for being a Judge for B.O.G. as well as a few pre-written stories—called Yarns or Serials if run in sequence. The other players will each play a single character in the Yarn (or multiple, should their first, or even second character die before the end of the adventure). Only Judges should read anything after page 39 until they have played a game or two.

Yet even though the Judge is, in effect, the spirit of the world, the rest of the group should be allowed and encouraged to add to the narrative; if Annabele the Frontier Settler wants to dive behind a large rock during a combat, let her. It doesn't matter that you, the Judge didn't describe it in the original scene—if it makes sense and it adds to the drama it should be allowed. If a player is shy or unsure, give them moments to shine—give them a hint if they are stuck or quiet the other players and allow her to speak if she feels as if she is being overridden; this game is about everyone having fun.

Additionally, the West is a harsh place and often deals with adult subjects, including the Yarns in the back of this book. If players or the Judge in the game are uncomfortable with these elements do not use them—the Judge should work to make an experience which is not only entertaining, but comfortable.

And since this world is so rough, it is not uncommon for a character to die, often unexpectedly and violently. Should this happen, it may seem like a prime opportunity to get upset—at the game, at the dice, or at the Judge—but this is wrong. Death and danger are a part of the game, and you can throw in with a new character in moments whose escapades can be just as humourous, exciting, or tragic as the last. Death is a part of life in the West, and embracing that is a core part of enjoying B.O.G.

Beyond all of this I have made every effort to be as sensitive as possible when approaching a world which rhymes with the American West. In pursuit of this, I felt it was impossible to avoid the difficult history resulting from the expansionism of the United States. Astute readers will note that both sects of Galugism in the chapter on Ludt include a saint whose primary domains include colonialism; this should be an indication that the N.L.P. is far from heroic, despite the fact that heroes may be N.L.P. citizens. I have made every effort to make the native tribes of Ludt as respectful to and distinct from specific native tribes in our world as possible, and to be sensitive both to their culture and to their history. It is important to me to acknowledge the controversies of the American West as much as to celebrate the media genre which has inspired B.O.G.

To play the game players will need notecards or sticky notes and a pen, both to record their characters and to report combat actions to the Judge, and as many six-sided dice (or d6s) as they can get their hands on. D6s can be looted from nearly any common family board game if need be. The Judge should additionally have two ten-sided dice of different colours (which may be purchased online or at many hobby stores); when they are asked to be rolled they will be referred to as D%. When required, both dice are rolled, and the first number represents the tens place, while the second represents the ones (the Judge should decide which is which before rolling); for example, a 9 and a 1 would be a 91.

Should a 0 be rolled on both dice, the result is a 100. Dice introduce an element of uncertainty into the game, and can also give the players a sense of accomplishment when they snatch their fate away from the jaws of death with an impressive roll.

At the end of the book is a story titled, <u>A City Man</u>. I am very proud of this story, and was happy to be able to write something which, to me, felt right at home in the faux-West I have fashioned. Anyone who is planning to be a Judge for B.O.G. can get unique inspiration from it, and I encourage them to do so. But if you are a player, you should wait until you have played a game or two before you dive in—there are some things in Ludt which are better to discover for yourself through play.

B.O.G. is a game about having fun while telling grim stories. It is a game about perseverance and survival. It is a game about sixguns and stagecoaches. But most importantly, it is <u>your</u> game. Do what you will with it.

Get along now,

F. Killian

April 19th, 2020

I would like to offer a special thank you to all
of those who have played this game in the past, which
include but are not limited to: Colin Zurnieden, Ken
Tollefson, Sebastian Barth, Erik Gatzke, Russell Viner,
Kieran Kane, Nate J. Bakke, Lillie Smith, John Mark Al-
varez-Wallesverd, Andréas Asklepiódotou, Ross Jennings,
and Colin Larter. I would also like to thank my father,
for introducing me to Westerns, <u>The Dark Tower</u>, and role
-playing games, and Ross Jennings, for experimenting
with game design with me throughout our youth.

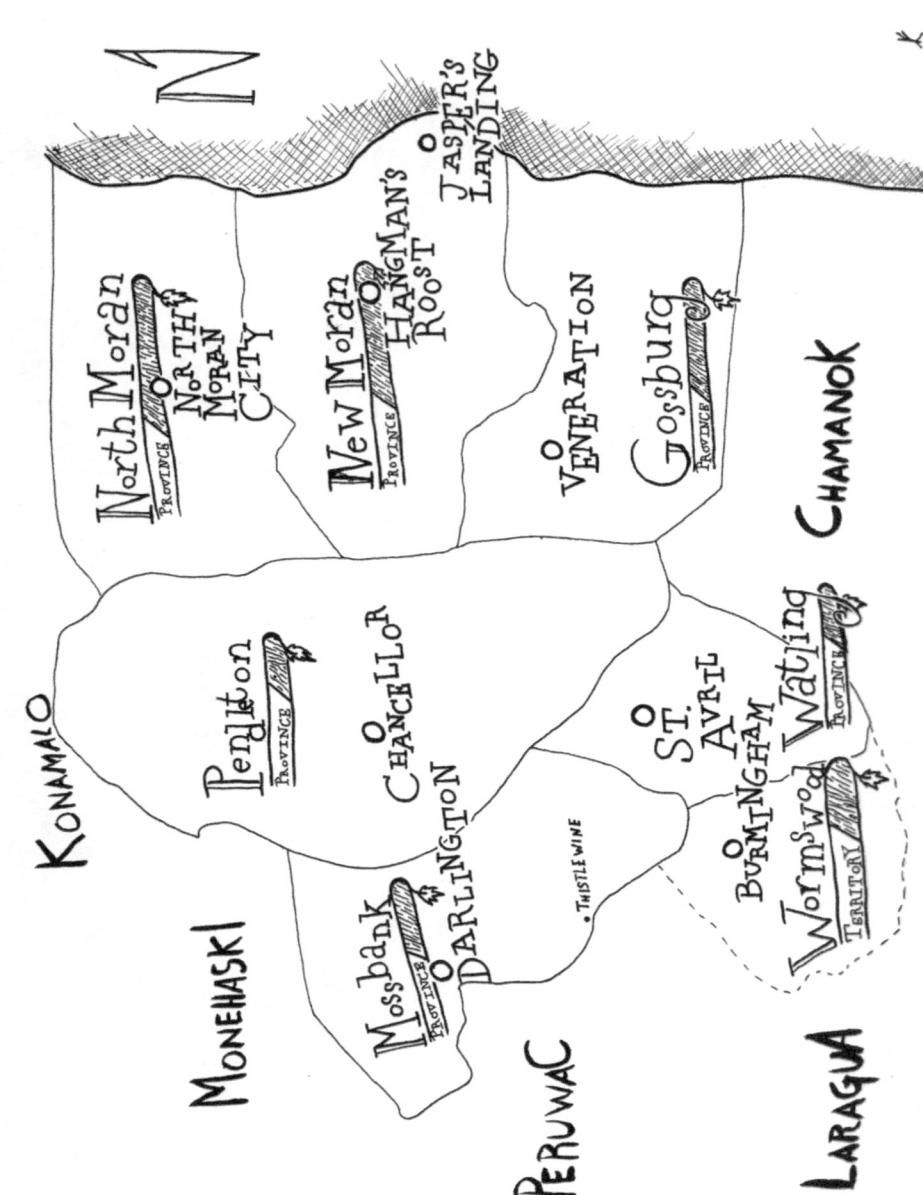

Ludt

Little true knowledge remains of the Old World across the Eastern Ocean, where once all the people of Ludt lived, for it has been many generations since any civilized man set foot there. What is known is that once there were many peoples, nations, and tribes which were settled on the archipelagos and pangaea-like central continent, whose histories stretched back for millenia.

A little over two hundred years ago Jasper Turnpike, a priest of the monotheistic church of Galugism (whose patron deity, Galug, was often referred to merely as the LORD) began to profess the evils of ancestor worship, which was a common practice, and called his followers to a holy war against the other peoples of that ancient world. The Jasperites, as they were called were soundly defeated, but their commander declared that there would be a message from Galug, proving the truth of his convictions and the sins of the false churches. The most loyal of the Jasperites built a fleet of thirteen ships and sailed west, never to see their home again. They landed on the shores of a new world after a harrowing journey and named it Ludt. In the decades which followed, what stragglers from the Old World came to join the new revealed that a terrible cataclysm had beset the forgotten continent, ravaging the land that was and reshaping it into an unlivable Hell. The Jasperites called this event the Great Judgement and saw it as the message they had expected from their LORD.

Ludt was not uninhabited, but the Jasperites claimed it nonetheless, by divine right, and began a steady progression west, pushing the native tribes further from the fertile and ancestral lands of the coast. In this colonized land the church established a governing body known as the N.L.P. - New Ludtish Provinces, operating out of the holy city of Jasper's Landing. The N.L.P. continues to press steadily westward, but a series of largely symbolic treaties with the native tribes have slowed the advance somewhat, when those treaties are not blatantly ignored.

A hundred years ago – and a hundred years after the Great Judgement, a descendant of Jasper Turnpike named Bartholomew Miter rose to prominence by his outspoken resistance to the theocratic governance of the N.L.P. Miter's resistance eventually grew to outright violence, and he and his adherents fought a two year long vigilante civil war against the government before finally being hanged. Yet after Miter's death, a new religious sect, canonizing him as a saint, arose and led a violent coup, which overthrew the government and instated a new, secular rulership of the Provinces.

This is the stage for Bone Orchard Gospel, two hundred years after the death of the Old World, as the N.L.P. Continues to expand its borders into the western frontier and the divides continue to grow between the religious and the secular, and the rich and the poor.

୭

JASPERISM

Jasperism is preached from a modified edition of the Book of Galug (though it is likely that no unmodified editions survived the Great Judgement), which professes the teachings and sins of the church, and includes fifteen Crucibles at the back – one for each of the Jasperist saints. Jasper's Landing is the most holy city of this sect, and is a common site of pilgrimage as well as commerce.

Priests of Jasperism wear a small, ship-shaped pin. The highest rank in the church is the Bishop-Practitioner, who is stationed in Jasper's Landing. Beneath the Bishop-Practitioner, each province has a bishop to oversee the theological activity of the territory, and each county in a province has a legate, and each town priest responds directly to their legate. Individual priests often devote themselves to the study of primarily one saint, but higher level theologians are usually versed in the theory of multiple saints.

The Thirteen Sins of Galugism:

♦ Murder, save as retribution

♦ Oathbreaking of any kind, with marriage vows being a common example

♦ Theft of property

♦ Worship of ancestors

♦ Cursing – both swearing and laying curses upon others

♦ Denying shelter or sustenance

♦ Reverence of goods, including being buried with valued objects

♦ Denial of the LORD

♦ Calling upon the LORD's name in vain

♦ A lying tongue

♦ Self-importance

♦ Betrayal of fellows

♦ The telling of half truths

The Fifteen Crucibles of Jasperism:

- ◆The Crucible of Jasper Turnpike - Patron Saint of Enlightenment

- ◆The Crucible of Crispin Adams - Patron Saint of Mercy

- ◆The Crucible of William Craw - Patron Saint of Retribution

- ◆The Crucible of Evangeline Drake - Patron Saint of Judgment

- ◆The Crucible of Amon Dadden - Patron Saint of Compassion

- ◆The Crucible of Wilmer Castleton - Patron Saint of Truth

- ◆The Crucible of Orville Emmet - Patron Saint of Humility

- ◆The Crucible of Lamen Thurch - Patron Saint of Loyalty

- ◆The Crucible of Avril Thatch - Patron Saint of Cultural Advancement and Colonialism

- ◆The Crucible of Auspice Murk - Patron Saint of Governance

- ◆The Crucible of Peter Thumb - Patron Saint of Sacrifice

- ◆The Crucible of Omen Wattle - Patron Saint of Art

- ◆The Crucible of Perthar Ockham - Patron Saint of the Inquisition

- ◆The Crucible of Laramie Booth - Patron Saint of Steadfastness

- ◆The Crucible of April Catch - Patron saint of Travel

 beta

MITERISM

The Miterist holy text is an even-further modified edition of the Book of Galug known as The Non-Secularist Book of Modern-Day Saints. This book follows the same general outline as the Jasperist text, though with a particular bias in the lessons towards the life and influence of Bartholomew Miter. The sins outlined are the same as for the Jasperists, and the first nine Crucibles are also shared. Two further saints are shared, but lived post-schism (Saints Omen and April), and Saint William has a different domain than in Miterism's sister religion. There are fourteen total Curcibles in Miterism. Jasper's Landing is a holy city for the Miterists, but so is Hangman's Roost, where Miter was hanged.

A vital part of the sect of Miterism, and the instigating event of the revolution which overthrew the theocratic government of the N.L.P., is the hanging of Saint Bartholomew and the so-called Six-Fold Retributions. When Miter was hanged he reportedly cried, "As I fall, so too falls the secular abomination of the Jasperist Church! There shall follow my hanging a pattern of six deaths in as many days – retributions on those who have wronged me and wronged our LORD!" There is some contention on which deaths were, in fact, the Six-Fold Retributions.

Priests of Miterism are identified by a ceremonial noose worn about their necks. The structure of their church is similar to that of the Jasperists, but their Bishop-Practitioner resides in Hangman's Roost. The Miterists also employ the fearsome marshal-inquisitors, which are discussed later under Governance and Enforcement.

The generally agreed-upon Six-Fold Retributions are (in

order):

♦Peter Thumb – The closest friend of of Saint Bartholomew, who betrayed him to the Jasperists and fell from his horse while being pursued by hounds

♦Thornbridge Cornwall – Saint Bartholomew's executioner, who was shot at his next execution by an unidentified assassin

♦Dallas Falks – The priest who placed the noose around Saint Bartholomew's Neck, who was shot by Oliver Silas – brother-in-law of Saint Bartholomew, who shot Father Dallas with the first six-chamber revolver

♦Bill Gursten – The Marshal of Denton County, who ordered the imprisonment of Saint Bartholomew and was struck in the head by a horse's hoof

♦Viktor Miel – The head of the N.L.P. Treasury, who was charged with unfair taxation and was stabbed through the heart in a duel with an anonymous Dovanri

♦Auspice Murk – Bishop-Practitioner of the Jasperist Church and Prince-Elect of the N.L.P. who was burned alive in the Grand Cathedral of Jasper's Landing in an unsolved arson

The Fourteen Crucibles of Miterism:

- The Crucible of Jasper Turnpike – Patron Saint of Enlightenment

- The Crucible of Crispin Adams – Patron Saint of Mercy

- The Crucible of William Craw – Patron Saint of Oaths

- The Crucible of Evangeline Drake – Patron Saint of Judgment

- The Crucible of Amon Dadden – Patron Saint of Compassion

- The Crucible of Wilmer Castleton – Patron Saint of Truth

- The Crucible of Orville Emmet – Patron Saint of Humility

- The Crucible of Lamen Thurch – Patron Saint of Loyalty

- The Crucible of Avril Thatch – Patron Saint of Cultural Advancement and Colonialism

- The Crucible of Bartholomew Miter – Patron Saint of Cleansing

- The Crucible of Omen Wattle – Patron Saint of Art

- The Crucible of April Catch – Patron saint of Travel

- The Crucible of Garl Jakes – Patron Saint of Burials

- The Crucible of Lamont Ult – Patron Saint of the Inquisition

❧

THE PEOPLES AND CULTURES OF LUDT

There were many nationalities, cultures, and ethnicities in the Old World, but under the rule of the

Jasperists these distinctions were largely eliminated, with all of those following their prophet acrost the ocean becoming one people. For this reason there are many distinct appearances to the peoples of the N.L.P., but with a few exceptions there is little racial friction inside of the Provinces, with most conflict being caused by class or religious differences. The major exceptions to this are the oppressed native tribes of Ludt – who are varied and honourable, but looked upon as savages and problematic obstructions to progress by the colonizing force of the N.L.P. – and the Dovanri, who are a race of nomads who came to Ludt from the ruins of the Old World after the rise of Miterism and have many strange ways and traditions, which often make them pariahs in Galugist society.

Of particular note to players is also the matter of language; vulgarity is improper and sinful. A civilized man using profanity is unacceptable, a woman using such language is beyond even this (being nigh unimaginable), and a constantly foul-mouthed character is not respected. In the country and on the frontier it is sometimes (<u>rarely</u>) used for emphasis.

⚮

GOVERNMENT AND ENFORCEMENT

The N.L.P. Is ruled by the non-hereditary position of <u>Prince-Elect</u> (which at one time was always held by the Jasperite Bishop-Practitioner) with a seat in Jasper's Landing. The Prince-Elect has fifteen <u>councilors</u> beneath him who, upon his death or dismissal (which is also at their discretion), elect a new Prince-Elect. Councilors are chosen via election upon their death, and votes are given to a random selection of twenty percent of the N.L.P. population, though these votes generally tend to be distributed throughout the more populous cities, and it is often suspected that higher net-worth individuals are given preference. Each province has a <u>mag-</u>

istrate appointed by the Prince-Elect, who oversees the administration of the various counties and law-enforcement therein. Each county is further overseen by a board of governors who are elected every five years by popular vote held in the county capital.

Each county's law-enforcement is overseen by a marshal, who reports directly to the provincial magistrate. Marshals are largely only involved in major cases which travel outside the jurisdiction of individual towns' sheriffs. Federal agents can be dispatched anywhere in the N.L.P., but only to monitor things which the N.L.P. Has direct jurisdiction over, such as collected tax money or census data - they are unable to pursue most crimes, and must often enlist the help of marshals, functionals, or the military to resolve complicated situations. The military of the N.L.P. technically has no power of law enforcement or governance, but on the frontier this restriction can sometimes be blurred; military detachments are normally dispatched to accompany federal agents or to pursue campaigns against the native tribes and in pursuit of colonial expansion. For crimes which cross provincial borders, the N.L.P. is required to rely on the assistance of the so-called functionals, independent contractors which are paid to collect bounties and pursue fugitives which fall outside of federal or magisterial jurisdictions; there are various organizations which these individuals work under, such as the famed Acquisitions Union based out of Chancellor. Finally, the Miterists deploy their own specific brand of enforcement known as the marshal-inquisitors, who seek out and punish heresy, blasphemy, and (primarily) theocratic interference in secular governance; the Jasperists also deploy inquisitors on occasion, though their powers are significantly reduced compared to the power of the mar-shal-inquisitors, who have full judgment in the sentenc-ing of convicted <u>secular-heretics</u>. Lawmen of all of the above ranks save functional have the power to deputize others to aid them in their efforts, but this is often considered carefully; additionally, compliance is not mandatory, and someone offered a deputyship may refuse.

Many large towns have a local <u>judge</u> which will oversee small legal matters. Should a case prove too volatile or complex for a local judge (who is often of middling ability and experience, though of great age), it may be transferred up to the <u>county courts</u>, and from there potentially to the <u>provincial courts</u>. There are no federal courts, but in the rare case where a provin-cial judge does not feel qualified to pass judgement they may hold conference with their peers or—in extreme-ly rare instances—ask for a ruling from the Prince-Elect himself.

જી

CURRENCY

Transactions in the N.L.P. are primarily made us-ing the exchange of <u>federal notes</u> (or merely notes). This paper currency is backed by gold held either in the provincial treasury or the national treasury, and often national notes are required when traveling outside of ones' own province; this usually requires paying a bank to change the money. Notes vary in size and design by mint of origin, but are often quite large, being an of-ficial writ of property owned. Occasionally silver or gold coins will be printed as well, and businesses or wealthy individuals may be entrusted with checks or a line of credit by their bank. For a fee, some courier services will also forward cash from one depot to anoth-er.

Other, smaller divisions of these notes exist, such as a <u>hundredth</u> (often called a dreth or a pfennig) which is a hundredth of a note, or a <u>bit</u> which is twelve and a half pfennigs.

Tracking currency in exact measures in B.O.G. is often unnecessary—you either have the money or you don't—but it can be entertaining and engaging to throw around concrete amounts. The Judge is encouraged to approximate when necessary. All references to notes in this text are denoted with a $.

Some example prices for reference are: a good horse for $200, a muzzle-loader rifle for $8, a shack for $25 or a four-room house for $700, a seat on a coach for a Bit per mile, or a drink for a Bit or sometimes two.

03

THE CALENDAR

Undoubtedly the people of the N.L.P. have their own unique calendar and system of naming for the days, but in interests of readability and engagement for players, all months and days are presented in terms of the English Gregorian calendar. Judges are encouraged to devise appropriate holidays as needed. No years are given, and should a Judge feel a need to come up with a system of exact dating they are encouraged to do so, though I have found it effective to refer to things rather in vague terms such as 'ten years ago,' etc.

03

ECOLOGY

Unless otherwise stated (or desired by the Judge) the environments of the N.L.P. are comparable to that of Earth's North America, with the Western provinces becoming more arid and wild and the East being greener and more tamed.

ଔ

COMMUNICATION

Letters, distributed by county postal services or by courier, are common, as are telegrams (a relatively new but incredibly popular technology).

ଔ

TRANSPORT

Common modes of transport are by horse, coach (being much safer over long distances than horse) or train where applicable. Automobiles are a relatively recent addition and are only owned by the wealthiest citizens; they are also not particularly suited to the rough roads outside of big cities, and so are usually used for local perambulation. Automobiles are primarily produced by the Avery Dane Motorcarriage Company, though other, smaller manufacturers do exist. Further, various powerful railroad companies populate the N.L.P., including the J.L. Montegue line and Vespers & Millin line (which compete for control of the West), Goodman East (which dominates the Eastern coastline), and the H.L.L. (Holy LORD's Line, which is owned and operated by a division of the Jasperist church, much to the Miterists' chagrin).

ଔ

THE MAP

The map included in this book shows the current provinces of the N.L.P., with capitals marked prominently. Wormswood Territory is also included, and will one day become a full province. Along the edges of the map are shown the native tribes which dominate those areas, and a mark is made for the location of Thistlewine, the small town used in the Yarns at the back of the book.

The provinces (and their capitals) are as follows: Gossburg (Veneration), Mossbank (Darlington), New Moran

(Jasper's Landing), North Moran (North Moran City), Pendleton (Chancellor), and Watling (St. Avril). The capital of Wormswood Territory is Burmingham.

The listed tribes are: the Chamanok, Konamalo, La-ragua, Monahaski, and Peruwac. There are countless sub-tribes inside of each of these, and there are likely other tribes which exist within the already colonized provinces of the N.L.P.

There are purposefully no defined geographical features on the map, besides on the eastern coast, as this should be up to the needs of the Judge to deter-mine; if the Judge desires a mountain range on the northern border of New Moran it can exist there for them, but it may not exist for another Judge.

Troopers, Vaqueros, and City Men

Each player in B.O.G. takes on the role of an individual character in the ongoing story. These may be any sort of person the players and Judge agree may be feasibly found in the Wild West of Ludt. Creating a character to play takes very little time, and should usually be done after the Judge introduces the scenario, so the players may use the circumstances as inspiration.

൪

CONCEPT

The player must devise a <u>Concept</u> for their character. A Concept may be what the character does for a living, or it may be a way of life, or a mannerism or feature which defines them. This can be drawn from western films or literature, the setting article at the start of the book, or historical knowledge of the North American West. Examples may be Sheriff, Train Robber, Functional, Priest, Native Tracker, Town Doctor, or any number of other appropriate professions. During play you may call upon their Concept for certain bonuses (with the Judge's approval); this is discussed in the chapter titled <u>A Fistful of Bones</u>.

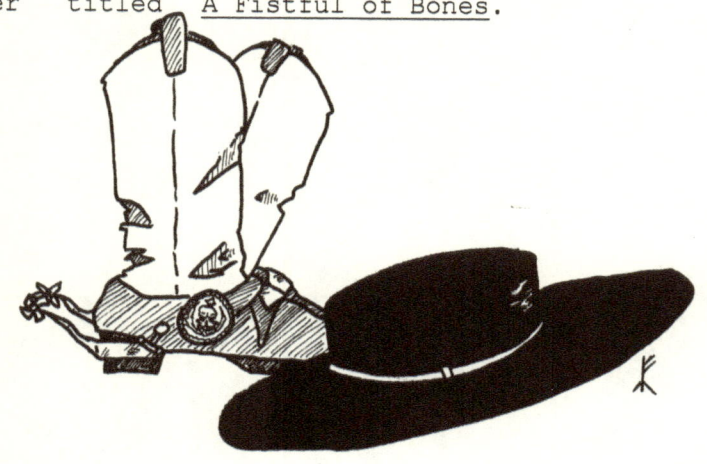

FEATURES

Every character has four <u>Features</u> which define their character and determine their capability at various tasks. These are determined by distributing 12 points between them. No Feature may have more than 5 points assigned to it, though Features may have 0 points assigned—that character will, however, be especially incapable at actions related to that part of themselves.

Features:

♦<u>Gumption</u>—A measure of a character's personal initiative, bravery, and strength of character and mind. Gumption is rolled whenever the character must confront their own psyche or think quickly. Of the Features, Gumption is rolled more often than the others outside of combat.

♦<u>Civilization</u>—A character's breeding and culture. Civilization is rolled in any situation involving etiquette. Using legalese to achieve a character's ends is also a legitimate use of Civilization.

♦<u>Grit</u>—How tough a character is, and how good they are in a fight, as well as their strength of body. Grit is rolled whenever physical prowess is tested.

♦<u>Learnin'</u>—A blanket term which encompasses all of a character's accumulated knowledge. Learnin' is rolled for any attempt to recall a piece of information your character may have gathered earlier in their life, such as subjects studied or things told to them.

Note that it is rare for a character to have both high Grit and high Civilization, as they represent two fundamentally opposite types of folk in the setting—cityfolk and countryfolk. Unless the Judge allows you to waive the restriction, only one of the two may be assigned points above 3.

ುಖ

FINISHING TOUCHES

The final step in creating a character is to flesh them out. Give them a name, a physical description, an age, and maybe a few detail about their life. The Judge will give the character any equipment which he finds to be appropriate for their Concept. Through play, the Judge may approve further equipment which it makes sense for the character to own, and which they conceivably have access to.

A Fistful of Bones

When a character attempts an action which has a reasonable chance of failure, or where failure would have dramatic influence on the story, the Judge may call for a roll. The Judge will declare which Feature is most appropriate to the situation and the player will roll a number of d6s equal to twice their Feature, comparing their best <u>Match</u> to a difficulty set by the Judge. A Match is string of the same number.

For example, if a character with a Feature of 4 were to roll, they would roll 8 dice. If the results are 1, 2, 2, 5, 5, 5, 5, and 6, the best Match would be 4 (since they rolled four 5s). The actual value of the rolled dice does not matter, only how many times each result was rolled.

If a player rolls, and achieves a Match 1 point lower than what is required, the Judge may choose to allow them a partial success, achieving only part of the intended goal with the intention of moving the story forward. This should not be used universally, but can help to avoid frustration from players and create new, interesting complications.

Should a player roll and achieve no Matches at all, the result is a catastrophic failure, with results determined by the Judge.

If two characters are opposing each other, such as in a game of cards or a horse chase, each side makes a roll, and whoever gains the better Match succeeds at their goal.

A character with appropriate experience (most probably through their Concept) may add 1 to the value of their chosen Match (in the above example the roll would count as a Match 5 rather than a Match 4).

Most rolls will be Match 4 rolls. Occasionally, easy rolls which the Judge feels still have a meaningful chance of failure may be Match 3. Difficult rolls should be Match 5 or even Match 6. Requiring Matches higher than 6 should be avoided outside of combat (where range can increase the chance of failure greatly or make it impossible).

⋈

COPPERING A FEATURE

A character may <u>Copper a Feature</u> in order to roll more dice. In doing so they raise their Feature by any amount equal to or less than the Feature's original rating before making the roll. If the roll succeeds, the Feature immediately reverts to its original value. If the roll fails, the Feature is reduced by the Coppered amount. Features lowered by Coppering regenerate at a rate of 1 point per week until it again reaches its original value. This loss of value represents a shattering loss of confidence—they put it all on the line and they lost; their gut was wrong and they need to come to terms with that.

⋈

LENDING A HAND

Occasionally the Judge may rule that a roll may be aided by one or more other character. Each helping character may roll a d6 and attempt to roll less than or equal to their appropriate Feature. On a success, they add 1 to the value of the primary roller's Match (hence, a Match 3 becomes a Match 4, etc.).

☙

COWARDS AND WANNABES

If, through play, a character does something which the Judge feels is especially against one of their Features (such as a high Gumption character fleeing from a fight) the Judge may ask them to make a Match 4 roll with that Feature. Failure results in the Feature lowering by one point; this point returns at the end of one week.

☙

NON-PLAYER CHARACTERS

Characters played by the Judge may not copper features, but may benefit from Concepts.

Buckets of Blood

Characters will inevitably come into conflict with their enemies. Combat in B.O.G. is incredibly deadly, and even a trained marksman may find himself felled by a stray bullet; in many instances it is preferable for characters to avoid armed conflict as avidly as possible. Keep in mind however, that most N.P.C.s are just as anxious about the concept as the player characters, and will take efforts to angle a conflict in their favour, or avoid blows if they see themselves at a disadvantage.

Combat in B.O.G. is divided into rounds, each of an undefined length of time—a single round could easily represent 1 second of action, or 20. On a round each  player with a participating character writes down the single action they wish to undertake on a slip of paper and hands it to the Judge. The Judge also secretly decides (before viewing the players' actions) what all N.P.C.s will do in the round. (NOTE: Conditional statements should be avoided in combat, as the action declared is an action undertaken no matter the circumstances.) Once all actions have been determined the Judge reads each of them and describes what occurs in the round, with all actions being resolved simultaneously.

It is up to the Judge how many shots can be fired from a firearm before it must be reloaded, but generally it is one unless using a revolver or a coach gun.

Grit is rolled in order to land a blow in combat, while Gumption is rolled to land a blow in a duel or if the opponent is unaware of the character. In melee, any Match of 4 or greater hits, while in ranged combat each 30' beyond the first increases the required Match by 1. Taking cover from ranged fire increases the opponent's required Match by an amount determined by the Judge. A target which declared they are moving in a round increases the required Match to hit them by 1 in that round against both ranged and melee attacks.

A hit results in a d6 being rolled on the appropriate damage table (presented later in the chapter), and the Judge is encouraged to devise more tables for weapons or damage types not represented. Some damage results also include a percentage chance; this is rolled against using a d%, and a failure (rolling equal to or less than the percentage listed) results in the character falling unconscious for the remainder of the scene.

Wounds should each be recorded separately, because each heals individually. Characters take penalties to all rolls based on how wounded they are, with each point of injury reducing the total number of dice rolled by that amount. All wounds are cumulative. A character who would roll 0 dice is incapacitated in regards to that Feature. Wounds are classified in three classes, given below with their name, penalty, and the amount of time it takes to heal if given appropriate care (wounds cannot heal without care):

Wound Class	Penalty	Healing time
Minour	1	1 Day
Moderate	2	1 Week
Severe	3	1 Month

ᘒ

QUICK DRAW

Should a character begin combat with a holstered pistol, they may attempt to draw and shoot it in the same action. This is a Match 5 Gumption roll (rather than a Match 4 Grit), further adjusted by cover and range.

ᘒ

ENVIRONMENTAL DANGERS

Environmental dangers (such as heat, drowning, fire, or extreme cold) can cause rolls on their own damage tables.

A drowning roll should be made every round until a drowning character is rescued. If a character falls unconscious from being water-logged and is not rescued and emptied of water in 1d6 rounds they shall die.

Poison rolls should be made immediately when the toxin is ingested or otherwise activated.

Cold and heat rolls should be made at the end of every day in which the character was exposed for at least 6 hours. If <u>frostbite</u> is untreated it will result in a loss of digits. Unconsciousness from temperature-related damage lasts for the entire next day. Further-more, each day after the first while still suffering from the wound's penalties requires the character to make a Grit roll to avoid losing another day. Appropriate clothing will allow a character to avoid a roll on the table unless exposed for at least 10 hours in a day.

☙

DAMAGE TABLES

HEAT			COLD		
1.	Sweating		1.	Runny Nose	
2.	Dehydrated	Minour 15%	2.	Chilled	05%
			3.	Frostbitten	Minour 30%
3.	Heat Exhaus-tion	Moderate 35%	4.	Frozen	Moderate 20%
4.	Desert Fevre	Severe	5.	Pneumonia	Severe 45%
			6.	DEAD	
5-6.	DEAD				

PISTOLS

1. Graze
2. Hit   Minour 05%
3. Good Shot   Moderate 10%
4. Serious   Severe 50%
   Wound
5-6. DEAD

SHOTGUNS

1. Good Hit   Moderate 20%
2. Serious Wound   Severe 40%
3. Serious Wound   Severe 60%

4-6. DEAD

Targets further than 30'
away cannot be hit, but
each time the shotgun is
fired damage is rolled
(individually) for each of

RIFLES

1. Graze
2. Hit   Minour 05%
3. Good Shot   Moderate 10%
4. Serious Wound Severe 50%
5-6. DEAD

Range increments are in
multiples of 100', rather
than 30'.

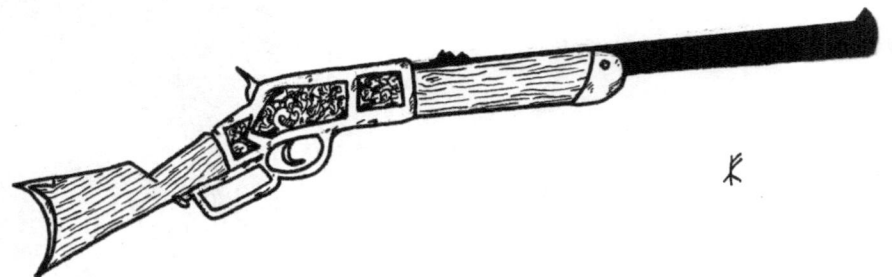

EDGED MELEE

1.	Hit	Minour 05%
2.	Hit	Minour 15%
3.	Good Hit	Moderate 50%
4.	Serious Wound	Severe 80%
5-6.	DEAD	

BLUNT MELEE

1.	Hit	Minour 05%
2.	Good Hit	Moderate 15%
3.	Broken Bone	Severe 25%
4.	Broken Bone	Severe 25%
5.	Concussed	Severe 75%
6.	DEAD	

Thrown Blades

1.	Wrong End	
2.	Hit	Minour 15%
3.	Good Hit	Moderate 35%
4.	Serious Wound	Severe 80%
5-6.	DEAD	

Bows

1.	Graze	
2.	Hit	Minour 15%
3.	Good Shot	Moderate 20%
4.	Serious Wound	Severe 40%
5.	Serious Wound	Severe 60%
6.	DEAD	

Range increments are in multiples of 50', rather than 30'. Also, it does not take an action to reload.

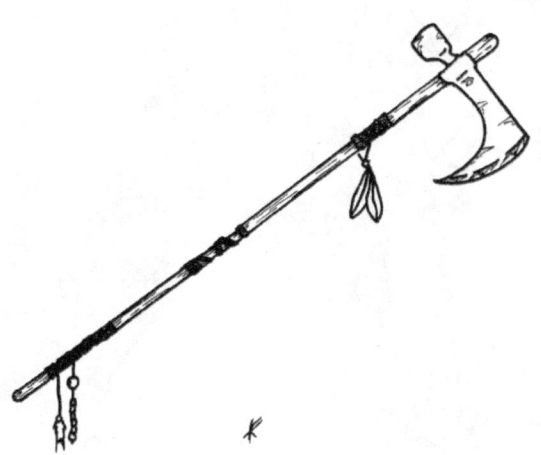

BRAWLING

1. Whiff
2. Hit   Minour 05%
3. Good Hit   Moderate 15%
4. Broken Bone Severe 25%
5. Concussed   Severe 75%
6. DEAD

STRANGULATION

1. Unaffected
2. Restrained   05%
3. Choked   Minour 30%
4. Bruised   Moderate
   Throat   45%
5. Briefly   Severe 100%
   Dead
6. DEAD

POISON

1. Unaffected
2. Upset Stomach Minour
   05%
3. Violently Ill Moderate
   10%
4. Fevred   Severe
   25%

5-6. DEAD

FALLING

1. Bruised   Minour
2. Solid Contact   Moderate
3. Solid Contact   Moderate
                   05%
4. Broken Bone   Severe 15%
5. Broken Bone   Severe 30%
6. DEAD

Roll once for every 10' of uncontrolled fall.

DROWNING

1. Holding Breath
2. Gasping
3. Taking Water   Minour
4. Suffocating   Minour 30%
5. Lungs Filled   Moderate

6. Water-Logged   Moderate
                   100%

FIRE

1.   Untouched
2.   Scalded
3-4. Light Burns   Minour
5.   Moderate   Moder-
      Burns   ate 15%
6.   Serious Burns   Severe
                      50%

Boomin' Along

B.O.G. is not a game meant for long campaigns, playing session after session of an ongoing story. Yet occasionally a Judge may run a few connected Yarns or allow a character who survived a previous one to join in a new adventure.

In these rare cases the Judge should allow the players to ask for one additional Skill to be added to their character which will function in the same manner as a Concept; Skills should cover a much more specific ability than the suite covered by Concepts, such as Dead Shot to aid in using firearms in combat. The benefits of Skills may be combined with those of Concepts for greater effect.

Additionally, each character transferring from one Yarn to the next may raise one Feature by 1 point if they allow the Judge to lower one of their other Features by 1 point; both of these changes must be supported by the actions of the characters during play. Further details on how the game is run over multiple sessions is discussed in the chapter All Manner of Yarns.

If you are not planning to fill the role of Judge

READ NO FURTHER

Until after you have played your first Yarn

If you are not planning to fill the role of Judge

READ NO FURTHER

Until after you have played your first Yarn

The Dry Blazes

You have been lied to.

This book opens by telling you not to expect things to appear in this game which are unrealistic in our, material world. It is true that this should not be expected, but the dire, occult, and supernatural is certainly present in Ludt, boiling and screaming and thrusting vilely beneath the thin skin of the world. First time players should not be aware of this, but the Judge should be, and should decide what that means for his version of the N.L.P. and environs.

The exact shape of this unpleasantness should be decided by each Judge, to match their specific flavour of Weird West, but the content which follows this chapter in the book gives an idea of the flavour with whose intention the book was written. The Yarns presented herein are each progressively more supernatural, and the short story A City Man offers insight into another part of the mysteries. The Book of Autumn, which is described in The Villains' Bible is a resource which could lead to more exciting and esoteric adventures.

Judges should also be meticulous in their presentation of the supernatural, and be certain to keep it as hidden as possible. While there will often be supernatural elements in many pre-written scenarios, it should be totally possible (and even probable) to solve most scenarios without discovering the dark underbelly. City Dogs is an excellent example of this, and even The Villains' Bible, while likely to at least arouse suspicion in the investigators, may result in the characters avoiding encountering irrefutable evidence of the esoteric.

For inspiration for this face of the game I encourage Judges to turn to the likes of H.P. Lovecraft, Robert W. Chambers, Stephen King, China Miéville, Robert E. Howard, and Clive Barker. I would be lying if I claimed these weren't my primary influences for this entire game, even the more mundane parts. But don't tell your players that.

☙

BRAVERY

When faced with the horrific or unknowable the Judge may call for a Match 4 Gumption roll. This is referred to in Yarn texts as a <u>Bravery roll</u>. Failing this test results in a brief loss of control, during which the Judge will dictate the actions of the character to correspond with their recent lapse in sanity; this could cause a character to flee, faint, or act irrationally. Achieving 0 Matches will result in long-lasting trauma, such as delusions or psychosis which will plague the character for the rest of their life; this should be a disorder agreed upon between the Judge and player, so that it is both appropriate to the instigating instance and comfortable for the player to role-play.

Occasionally Bravery rolls may have a higher dif-ficuly than 4, but this should only be in instances with a distinct connection to the character—perhaps emotion-al, or perhaps in challenging a core tenet of their faith or way of life. Bravery rolls may also occasion-ally be used for non-supernatural instances, but this should be rare indeed, and only for something far afield of a character's concept; perhaps witnessing a bloody murder would require a Bravery roll from the daughter of a wealthy investor, but a miner or vaquero are used to the hard realities of life and may be upset and dis-turbed, but not enough to cause them to lose control.

All Manner of Yarns

Yarns in B.O.G. are generally told in three main forms, all of which are discussed here. Firstly, there are pre-prepared Yarns, such as <u>City Dogs</u>; these are prepared ahead of time and have a structure and anticipated outcome. Secondly, there are pick-up Yarns, where the Judge and the players decide to play the game and determine on the spot what the scenario should surround; these are generally less complex than pre-prepared Yarns and can easily lead to exciting and high-octane action scenes. Finally there are Serials, where a few pre-prepared scenarios are run in sequence, over the course of multiple nights.

In all of these types of Yarns it is important to keep in mind how easy it is to create characters for B.O.G. This is a vital part of how B.O.G. is played; if a character dies and there is still a significant amount of the Yarn remaining, that player should be allowed to create a new character and introduce it into play whenever the Judge sees fit. This is an especially vital part of pick-up Yarns, as discussed below.

Pre-written Yarns may either be taken from official B.O.G. supplements or written by an individual Judge. They have a defined goal and anticipated series of events. Often they include a hint of the supernatural, sometimes hidden and avoidable, and sometimes blatant and confrontational. Additionally, sometimes pre-written Yarns state events or outcomes as fact, but it is important to always allow the players the ability to change those events and outcomes or avoid them; for example, at the end of <u>The Villains' Bible</u> it is stated that the Miterists do not gain any confiscated items from the raided printing press, yet if a player is playing a Miterist with any amount of authority they may alter this apparent inevitability. Yarns in this book can serve as good examples of a pre-written Yarn.

Pick-up Yarns are in many ways the opposite of pre-written Yarns, but are also the source of many of the most memorable moments from B.O.G. games. A pick-up Yarn begins when a group of players sits down and decides to play B.O.G. without pre-planning. One of the players is nominated to act as Judge, and the group decides communally what the scenario should focus around—a train robbery, a bank heist, a confrontation with the natives, a military takeover of a frontier town, a trial of secular-heretics, etc. Each player makes a character appropriate to the scenario and play begins, with the Judge holding the framework together. A pick-up Yarn is played until the group decides that it has satisfactorily concluded. These stories should usually be high energy and volatile situations, and if a character dies their player should immediately step into the shoes of another character already at the scene; it is often entertaining for a character to die and then create a character on the opposing side. In one infamous pick-up game the players began as train robbers, and by the end they were all playing military guards onboard the train trying to fend off the last of the bandits! One important note about pick-up games is that they should generally not include supernatural elements; the supernatural in B.O.G. is a very thematic element which should never be included lightly, and should be carefully planned to preserve the terror and mystery behind it— have fun in the Old West for these games, and leave the Weird West for another night.

B.O.G. is not a game meant to be played over a long period of time, as stated earlier, but occasionally a character will take part in two, or even three, connected Yarns in a row. These are called Serials. Serials use the character advancement rules from Boomin' Along and usually have a connected story throughout each pre-written adventure. The three Yarns in this book to-gether form the <u>Gaff County</u> Serial (even though <u>The Vil-lains' Bible</u> barely takes place at all in Gaff County), though they can be run individually or as only two parts, at the Judge's option. As Serials are composed of pre-written Yarns, the guidelines for those types of stories should generally be followed.

City Dogs

City Dogs is a Yarn which takes place in Gaff County in Mossbank Province, the most recent and most westerly of the N.L.P. Provinces. It may be played as a stand-alone tale, or may be continued in a further session with The Villains' Bible. The action opens in the small town of Thistlewine, where a young banker has been murdered, ostensibly by the local Peruwac tribe of natives; supply this information to the players before they create their characters to give them inspiration for their Concepts. It is suggested that the characters arrive by coach at the designated time in the adventure, rather than already being there; this is not necessary, but the adventure may need some adjustment if the characters are natives.

THE SCENE

Thistlewine is a small mining burg near the border with the expansive native wilderness to the west. No railroad lines run through Thistlewine. This little town is the last vestige of civilized life before entering the lands of the Peruwac.

It is early August and 'hot as a whorehouse on nickel night' when a young banker departs a coach at the edge of Thistlewine. Word spreads quickly that he has come from Chancellor out East (Chancellor is the capital of Pendleton Province and by many is considered the greatest city of the West, though in the truly western provinces of Mossbank and Watling it is considered securely Eastern). The man's name is Darius Autumn and he rents a room at The Bull's Sink, the only watering hole in Thistlewine. It is unclear why he is here, and the old folk talk. Autumn stays for two weeks and then is murdered. The party arrives by coach a week later.

Upon arriving in town the characters are made aware that the local sheriff, Peter Salt, has offered a $300 reward for the capture and incarceration of the murderers. The killing is still the talk of the town, and the players should have no trouble making their way to Sheriff Salt's office. Most townsfolk are superstitious about the natives; they of course all blame the Peruwac and will spread all manner of inaccurate and often mystical rumours about the foul abilities and intentions of their neighbors. If the players make clear their intention to investigate the bounty, Salt will offer to deputize them, but still allow them to keep the reward; he is relieved to have such a potentially volatile case taken off his hands and he wants it resolved as quickly and simply as possible.

The Sheriff will describe to them how Darius was thrown from the second story of the inn last Monday with a bone native hunting knife stuck between his eyes; a feat requiring a suspect of exceptional strength. All of Autumn's possessions, which were contained in three valises and a steamer trunk) were stolen from his room, presumably through the window and over the roof (another feat of exceptional strength), as no one in the Sink saw anyone leave with them. Sheriff Salt will make especial mention of there being a pair of Peruwac in town around the same time who disappeared shortly before the murder; he strongly hints that he wouldn't mind the Peruwac ending up dead, should they be the guilty party.

If the party is lacking ideas as to what leads to follow, suggest a few options. Perhaps they could talk to the owner of the local inn, or examine the crime scene? It may be worth talking to the local bank and seeing if they had dealings with Darius. Where are the two missing Peruwac?

❧

THE BULL'S SINK

Bill Trenchant, the proprietor of the Bull's Sink, also believes that the Peruwac are to blame, and names them as the brother and sister pair known as Crawling Oxen and Triumphant Oak. The two often come into town and trade with the miners.

If asked about the events of the night or Darius's activity Trenchant will state that Darius spent much of his time in his room, and came down only to take his meals (which he brought back up to his chamber) or for occasional hikes around the outskirts of town. On the date of the murder, it was about 10a.m. when the proprietor heard the sounds of a struggle from above, in Autumn's room. He began for the stairs, but it was then that he heard the sound of the corpse hitting the porch awning outside, and crashing through. After seeing the body, he ran to find Sheriff Salt, after which he and Salt went upstairs to find the door locked. Entering it they found it empty.

Darius's room contains a bed, a writing desk, and a chair. The room has been left as it was found except that Trenchant has closed the window, which was found open, and faces the main street. Examining Darius's room reveals (with careful searching and perhaps a Match 4 Gumption roll) a crumpled slip of paper, discarded under the bed and smudged with coal dust. On the paper is a poorly written note:

Mister Ahtum,

We cant quiet make the payment yet. Moor time wood help.

The guests who were staying at the Sink have all passed on, but Trenchant can supply their names, professions, and general destinations. This is up to the Judge to include if needed, and may serve as a lead to a future Yarn, should the Judge choose not to continue this Serial with The Villains' Bible.

Trenchant's daughter, Maria, will tell them that two weeks ago a miner came and gave a note to her for Autumn. The miner's name was John Barns, and he lives with his cousins, Wilmer Digs and Carl Peterson, down by the mines a few miles out of town. The Barns Gang are all big men, who are proud of their ability to hurt people, and often openly carry weapons into town, though they do not visit often. They have an exceptionally foul reputation in Thistlewine.

Should any of the party be especially flirtatious it is worth noting that Maria is engaged, and fanatically loyal; they are truly in love.

ତ

BECKS AND O'SHANESY

The local bank, if interviewed, will confess that Barns and his cousins owe a significant amount to their establishment, but that they have no ties to Darius Autumn.

ତ

RELIGION IN THISTLEWINE

There is no church in Thistlewine, but most of the populace is staunchly Jasperist; they see the Miterist resistance to meddling as uncompassionate, and welcome any help offered by Jasperist missionaries.

THE PERUWAC

There is a Peruwac camp roughly ten miles west of Thistlewine, and anyone in town can easily point the way. Their chief is an old man named <u>Crying Pig</u>. The son of Crying Pig—<u>Braying Kine</u>—speaks some of the <u>civilized</u> tongue and will help translate for his father.

Crying Pig will say that Crawling Oxen and Triumphant Oak have been missing for two weeks. Search parties were sent out, but no trace has yet been found. Braying Kine will add that it is assumed amongst the tribe that the two ran away and eloped; he will be both amused and offended if the characters repeat the untruth they had previously been told that the pair were siblings. Triumphant Oak was engaged to another brave from the village, but refused to marry him. Crying Pig and Braying Kine will not allow the party to interview other members of the tribe.

If the characters imply that the lovers may be to blame for the murder they will be defended vehemently. If it is implied that they may have fallen prey to some ill fortune from the locals, Crying Pig will send the characters away and begin to prepare for a raid on Thistlewine. Braying Kine is a much more compassionate individual, and may potentially be reasoned with by the party to prevent hostilities; Braying Kine may even be persuaded (should his father stand down) to send four of the village's braves with the characters to investigate, on behalf of the tribe.

THE MINES

If the party goes to explore the mines (which are seven miles northwest of town and about 3 miles northeast of the Peruwac village), they will be confined there and forced to seek shelter by a lightning storm (which are fairly common here). There are many small caves and fissures in the area as well as the mine itself; attempting to make the mouth of the mine rather than a nearby instance of cover they risk being struck by lightning (as below). The miners have all returned home in anticipation of the storm. Anyone out in the storm for more than five minutes without seeking shelter is subject to a roll on the <u>Lightning Storm</u> damage table below if they fail a Match 3 Gumption roll; should the roll fail by only 1 point, the horse is struck instead, and may bolt or throw the rider from the saddle:

LIGHTNING STORM

1-3. Untouched

4. Shocked   Moderate 35%

5. Electrocuted Severe 70%

6. DEAD

While under cover they may glimpse Triumphant Oak walking out in the storm. She has been abused for days by Barns and his gang and is barely able to speak. She will manage to sob out 'Crawling Oxen… The cottage in the hills,", but no more; she is in desperate need of rest and care, both physically and emotionally. If the party calms her—likely through the use of drugs such as laudanum or perhaps some mixture of cocaine, she will mumble in Peruwac about three men and a hole in the ground. She will become agitated and attempt to escape or call out if she realizes she is being taken back to the shack. The cottage is not far from where the party has hidden, and her tracks can be easily followed.

Should the party wish to outlast the storm it will pass in about an hour.

ଊ

BARNS AND HIS GANG

Barns and his cousins are at home. They are an unsavoury crew, and will deny any charges if confronted. They will under no circumstances allow entrance to their hut. Should conflict arise use the below stats for each of the men. John Barns carries a rifle, as does Wilmer Digs. Carl Peterson carries a shotgun.

Gumption · · · · · · · · · · · · · · 5

Civilization · · · · · · · · · · 0

Grit · · · · · · · · · · · · · · · · 5

Learnin' · · · · · · · · · · · · · 2

The hut is only one room with three cots, a small table, a single chair, and a steamer trunk in one corner. Every surface in the home is littered with empty liquor bottles. The trunk is Darius Autumn's, and contains most of the banker's belongings—clothes, documents from his job with the Chancellor Great Bank (which say nothing about any dealings with Barns or his cousins), personal care items, etc. There is a trap door in the floor secured with a sturdy padlock, to which Barns holds the key.

If Barns and his fellows believe that they have been discovered, they will attempt to slay or knock out the characters and throw their bodies into the pit under the house. If any are captured alive they will admit to the slaying of Darius Autumn, saying that they had been dealing with 'him and his folk' for a year or more. They will admit to raping Triumphant Oak and to slaying her lover; Barns saw the two Peruwac in town when he went to deliver Darius the letter and decided then that he would take her. It was the Peruwacs' ill fortune in addition to this, that they witnessed the murder from the main street, prompting the Barns Gang to commit to both planned atrocities at the same instance. Additionally, removing the primary suspects from the picture would, in his mind, make it less likely to prove their innocence and thus distract attention from himself and his cousins. They will also admit to ambushing Autumn from his balcony and taking his belongings away via rooftop escape. They will under no circumstances betray their cult, and will go smiling to the hangman's noose.

The basement of the house, under the padlocked door, is a ten foot drop to an earthen floor. There are no stairs, ladder, nor rope to facilitate a descent. An unlit oil lamp is in the center of the soil floor and can be easily lit if retrieved. There is also a book with a black cover near the lamp; anyone coming into contact with the book feels distinctly uneasy; examining both it and the bank documents will reveal the same handwriting in both—presumably that of Darius Autumn. Also visible for those who peer through the hole in the floor with a light is the naked corpse of Crawling Oxen with his throat slit.

If the lantern in the pit is lit, there is a cracking noise from Crawling Oxen's corpse. Then, after about ten minutes of inaction, his back will arch, his arms will break backwards, and a forest of black, rib-like protrusions will burst from his stomach and, with a horrible screech, he will attack. Those hearing the screech or seeing the horror must make a Match 6 Bravery roll. It is entirely possible that the characters will not witness the horror of Crawling Oxen; the lantern is the incitement for the dark ritual attempted by the Barns Gang, and without its lighting the creature will not be awoken.

ʘ

THE TRUTH ABOUT JOHN BARNS

The Barns Gang is in fact a part of a much larger cult based out of Chancellor, and owes dues to Darius's

Uncle. John Barns purchased one of Darius Autumn's original copies of the manuscript from the banker's uncle on credit, but have spent all of their money gained since then on booze and whores; the cult head has threatened to collect. Darius, who had begun to become aware of his uncle's cult, had come to Thistlewine to attempt to gain more information and perhaps stymie his uncle's efforts, but he was slain by Barns and his cousins who mistakenly believed him to be a representative of his relative. These details are impossible to gather during the course of this Yarn, and the characters will likely devise their own, inaccurate conclusion. If the Judge wishes to explore this further they may continue the Serial with The Villains' Bible. Reading the book is a lengthy task, which is beyond the scope of City Dogs.

ভ

"CRAWLING OXEN"

Gumption · · · · · · · · · · · · · · 5

Civilization · · · · · · · · · · · 0

Grit · · · · · · · · · · · · · · · · 5

Learnin' · · · · · · · · · · · · · 0

ভ

THE RAID ON THISTLEWINE

If Crying Pig has been instigated to war, he will lead a raid on Thistlewine two days after his instigation. All able-bodied members of the tribe will attack the town. The conflict will be bloody and result in many deaths, but ultimately will likely result in the near total annihilation of the Peruwac village. Should this occur, it can be played out at the end of the adventure, or described narratively. The raid is fairly likely to happen, unless the party makes a concentrated effort to convince the Peruwac against it.

The Villains' Bible

The Villains' Bible is a Yarn which is meant to be played as the second part of a Serial along with City Dogs, but with some modification it can be run as a standalone Yarn. The adventure takes place some time after the events of City Dogs (the exact amount of time is up to the Judge, but when this was originally run it was twenty years, as one of the players—playing the Marshal of Gaff County—had devoted the remainder of his career to a vain search for more details on the strange book found in the basement of Barns's cabin), and begins with a letter being sent to the individual in possession of Darius Autumn's book, who ideally is still residing in or near Thistlewine.

CR

THE SCENE

A letter is delivered to the possessor of Darius Autumn's book. It is from Grover Autumn, Darius's uncle, and invites the character to meet him at his home in Chancellor to discuss new information which has come to light concerning his nephew's death.

❧

THE BOOK OF AUTUMN

The book which was found in John Barns's basement is referred to in this text, and by its adherents, as The Book of Autumn, though it bears no title when found. It is a modern occult masterpiece, originally handwritten multiple times over the course of a few fevred months by Darius Autumn and then secretly printed en masse and dispersed amongst the Order of Autumn by his uncle Grover. It is written in Shuggrak, a coded language invented by Darius Autumn, its author. Only a handful of people know Shuggrak, and no one in the Order of Autumn knows the true author of the book, save Grover Autumn. The book reveals many maddening secrets about the nature of Ludt, and claims that Ludt is in fact a mirror of the true world, and that someone in the N.L.P. is the true nexus of existence; the book calls this person the Lord of Ludt, but stops short of naming them in the final chapter, which was left unfinished.

The Book of Autumn is incredibly dangerous, and Darius regretted writing it as soon as his madness subsided—thus his leaving it unfinished. He did not know where the inspiration for his work came from. He was also unaware that his uncle had discovered it and begun production and distribution of it until it was too late.

The Order of Autumn itself is not organized, save for Grover Autumn and his most trusted aides, which include the Conway Gang—of which the small Barns Gang was an unproductive associate. Grover Autumn hopes to cause enough chaos that the Lord of Ludt is revealed to him and he may claim his power.

❧

THE CONWAY GANG

The party must first travel to Darlington, the capitol of Mossbank Province, where the J. L. Montegue railway line begins. Darlington is ninety miles north of Thistlewine. The most plausible means of reaching there is a five day passage on a coach, though other means could be explored, such as renting or buying horses, but this is of course a more dangerous route, possibly rife with bandits, raiders, or fierce predators. Once in Darlington it is a hundred and eighty miles to Chancellor, or three more days by rail. While stopped in Darlington the party witnesses an altercation caused by the Conway Gang—perhaps a barfight or an extortion.

The Conway Gang is from Trinian County in the south of Pendleton Province and is famous enough that anyone in the party may recognize them on sight with a Match 4 Learnin' roll. Their crimes are many, and there are standing bounties of upwards of $300 on each member, with $500 on Chuck Conway himself (see Conway Gang on page 63).

When boarding the train, characters will notice the Conway Gang also boarding with a Match 6 Gumption roll.

The train is staffed with a line constable and his three deputies, who act as legal authorities while on the line. Any individuals bringing weapons aboard are allowed to keep them, but must register them with the line constable and are expected to keep them stowed in the overhead shelf in their compartment.

At the first stop after Darlington—a small town called Podunk, which is barely more than the train station, the Conway Gang will enter the car with the players and begin violently threatening (and perhaps even killing or maiming) the other passengers in search of the holder of the book. Should they find the holder of the book they will shoot him and reclaim the book; if this happen the Yarn either ends or the Judge must contrive a new manner in which the remaining characters or their replacements will come into contact with Grover

Autumn.

Entering through the door between compartments I and V on the map below, Conway and his gang will begin with those two compartments. Compartments IV, V, and VII are empty. I holds a newly married couple. II holds a county judge and his three secretaries. III is the party's compartment. VI includes a lawyer, his wife, sister-in-law, and young son. VIII includes a retired marshal who is slumbering deeply. All compartment doors slide sideways, while the doors to the car open inwards.

The Conway Gang consists of Chuck Conway, Big Bill Saxon, Iseah Fontaigne, Felix Cochran, and Tom "The Axe" Barns (the brother of John Barns). Chuck carries a single-action pump rifle, as does Big Bill, though Big Bill also has a sixgun. Iseah Carries a double-barreled shotgun, as does Felix, who also carries a bowie knife. "The Axe" carries a hatchet and a two-shot derringer. All of them carry a boot knife.

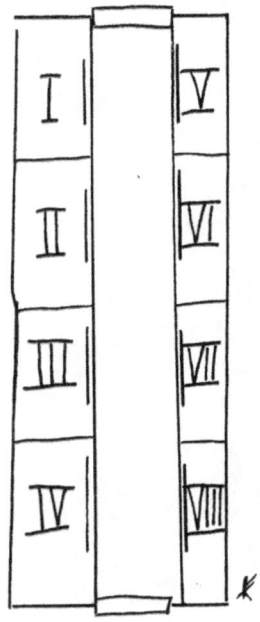

CHUCK

Gumption · · · · · · · · · · · · · · 5

Civilization · · · · · · · · · · 2

Grit · · · · · · · · · · · · · · · · 4

Learnin' · · · · · · · · · · · · · 1

BIG BILL

Gumption · · · · · · · · · · · · · · 5

Civilization · · · · · · · · · · 2

Grit · · · · · · · · · · · · · · · · 5

Learnin' · · · · · · · · · · · · · 0

ISEAH

Gumption · · · · · · · · · · · · · · 5

Civilization · · · · · · · · · · 3

Grit · · · · · · · · · · · · · · · · 2

Learnin' · · · · · · · · · · · · · 2

FELIX

Gumption · · · · · · · · · · · · · · 4

Civilization · · · · · · · · · · 1

Grit · · · · · · · · · · · · · · · · 4

Learnin' · · · · · · · · · · · · · 3

THE AXE

Gumption · · · · · · · · · · · · · · 5

Civilization · · · · · · · · · · 0

Grit · · · · · · · · · · · · · · · · 5

Learnin' · · · · · · · · · · · · ·2

Only Chuck knows anything beyond their employment— "Mr. Chuck don't take kindly to you folk talking to Mr. Autumn," is a stock phrase which could easily be used by any of the other gang members who are questioned—during the assault or after. Chuck was asked by Grover Autumn to remove the character who was in possession of the book from the picture. Conway also has been given an occult gift by his studies into the true nature of the world; he has a penchant for lying and may never fail a roll to do so. Astute observers may notice his black, forked tongue.

The line constable and his deputies will arrive on the sixth round of combat and will aid against the Conway Gang, attempting to subdue them rather than slay them if possible. Once Conway and his gang are slain or apprehended the line constable will offer to pay a part of the total bounty from the train's coffers and take the remainder as a fee when they return the Conways to the Darlington authorities. The line constable will be able to offer up to $1400 total.

⊂⊃

CHANCELLOR

Should the characters reach Chancellor they will be greeted by Grover Autumn, a dry, clean-cut man with an automobile—a brand new Dane Model 4 (a new and exciting invention!). The auto only fits four, including the driver, so if the party is larger than three individuals he will suggest that they walk and will retrieve the vehicle later.

Should the characters tell Grover of their conflict with the Conway Gang he will appear horrified, and will confess no knowledge of why they would do such a thing. He will profess his distaste with discussing such sordid news.

Mr. Autumn's estate is a gorgeous three story home in the wealthiest part of Chancellor. He will insist that the party wait until tomorrow to discuss his nephew, and if the assault on the train has been brought up he will use it as an excuse, saying that it has greatly upset him and he must take time to settle his nerves.

He will gladly discuss politics, and will communicate his largely socialist leanings, decrying the expansionism of the West. as driven by personal greed rather than rational economic concerns. He believes that ownership of business should be shared by its employees. As for expansion in the west, he supports independent settlers moving west, as they are more likely to live off the land rather than encourage increased corporate expansion and greed, and believes that western expansion gives a convenient avenue for larger companies which are unwilling to reform to relocate far from the reach of the law. Characters should make Match 4 Learnin' rolls to keep pace with Autumn's theorizing, and any religious person participating in conversation with him may be struck by how close he comes to blasphemy by denying the expansionist domains of St. Avril. He will argue, if challenged on the matter, that by supporting independent settlers he is still adhering to the teachings of St. Avril, though perhaps in a less orthodox manner than that generally adhered to by the N.L.P.

His wealth comes from his controlling share in the Chancellor Post He will have plenty of wine on hand (a Match 4 Civilization roll will reveal the impressive vintages) and his staff of four servants will serve three courses that evening.

The wine has been infused with a powerful drug, which requires a Match 5 Grit roll to resist; these rolls should be made secretly by the Judge. Failure results in an overwhelming sense of exhaustion which will swiftly lead to a deep sleep. Once the meal is done or and/or the characters have begun to nod off, Grover will lead the PCs to his guest bedrooms on the second floor.

During the night there will be a break-in. 10 heavily armed men in wooden fox masks will break down the front door and gather everyone in the house into a large motorcarriage, similar to those used by marshals during arrests, with a large covered back end with twin doors at the back, one of which holds the only window outside of the cab. Those who failed their rolls against the toxin will be unable to fight back. The fox -men will prefer to use non-lethal force if necessary, and so will use truncheons rather than their firearms or knives whenever possible. Use the same profile as for the Crawling Oxen horror from City Dogs on page 57 should conflict arise.

During the assault, before the party is forced into the wagon, the fox-men will cut out Grover's tongue and dispose of it.

The party will be brought to an abandoned train station on the other side of Chancellor, after which point all but two of the fox-men will leave, making escape a simple prospect. The train depot is enclosed by a steel domed framework with old, soot-stained and broken glass panels. The combat with the fox-men should not be simply resolved, but nonetheless should result in the characters emerging victorious; make them feel like they were challenged, even if minimally. [If the Judge does not intend to run The Wild Spirits of Gaff County after this Yarn, more fox-men may be left behind, and the difficulty of the encounter may be increased, even to a deadly level.] The other fox-men will return to Grover's home and burn it to the ground.

☙

GROVER AND THE FOX-MEN

The fox-men are operating under Grover's orders. They are occult constructions which he has brought to life using the mysteries of The Book of Autumn. Should the masks be removed from any of the fox-men they will be revealed to have had their faces removed and skulls hollowed out and filled with dried hemlock; this re- quires all witnesses to make a Match 4 Bravery roll. They were once victims of violence murdered by Grover's servants or fished from the Hagawonn River, which runs through Chancellor. Placing a fox-mask on a recently deceased corpse will re- turn it to life for one hour. This will only work once per corpse.

Grover's tongue will regrow in one week, but he will continue to pretend muteness. He will, how- ever, keep the details of his mutilation out of the news. This re- generation is an effect of his relationship with the occult. Additionally, all Wounds dealt to him count as minour, and should an attack on him miss he may voluntarily switch places with a fox-man anywhere in Chancellor. Witnessing any of Grover's supernatural powers for the first time will require a Match 4 Bravery roll. Grover's Features are all value 5. Unless slain (by a DEAD result on a damage table) Grover Autumn is effectively immortal.

Grover uses secret presses beneath the sewers to

print additional copies of The Book of Autumn using his fox-men as free labour. He had hoped to eliminate the threat to his growing Order of Autumn by sending Conway after the characters, but after that failed (should it have failed) he decided to mislead the characters instead. He is willing to sacrifice his current operation in order to mislead authorities and potential spread the text even further.

❧

AFTER THE ESCAPE

The party will likely want to take Grover Autumn to a hospital. The next day they will be able to speak with him, via his use of a pen and writing pad. He will affect tiredness after four questions from the party.

Grover will attempt to garner from the characters by claiming that the Conway Gang tried to kill his nephew, thus why he was so disturbed by the news on the train. He claims to know nothing of the book if questioned, and that he has never seen the fox-men before. Mr. Autumn will claim that Darius had no friends or family. He carries on him a key to the murdered man's house, which he bought after the murders and left untouched, and he will offer it as a potential lead.

❧

THE INVESTIGATION

Checking court records will reveal that Darius Autumn had a wife named Claudia, who was slain around the same time as her husband. If confronted about this, Grover will claim that he was not actually very close with his nephew.

The house is covered in a thick layer of dust, and it is obvious no one has been in here in years. If the house is searched, Claudia Autumn's diary can be found hidden inside her mattress. This diary details her fears concerning Darius, who attempted to explain to her what he was experiencing as he worked on his manuscript. At some point Darius's attitude changed and (according to the diary) he burned all of his notes. This is the best way for the characters to become aware of the true nature of the book and its author. Darius's room (separate from Claudia's) is in poor condition compared to the rest of the house, as the window was left open. In there can be found a letter from Chuck Conway requesting a copy of the book and threatening Claudia; this letter was in fact planted by order of Grover Autumn, and was written that day.

While the party is exploring the house it will be attacked by Chuck Conway, any surviving members of his gang, and a handful of fox-men. If Conway was slain earlier, he will have been resurrected using one of the fox masks. If he was imprisoned he will have been freed by an assault by fox-men on the jail. Either Conway or one of the fox-men will flee the combat, and can be tailed back to the secret print shop beneath sewers.

Should this be intended to be a standalone Yarn, or the end of the Serial, the authorities can help the party to track down Grover and apprehend or slay him. Should the Judge intend to run The Wild Spirits of Gaff County after this, however, the official blame will be placed squarely on Conway, and Grover will stand up for the party in court should the need arise. Regardless of the ending chosen, many of the copies of The Book of Autumn will be confiscated by the Jasperites (though the Miterists will unsuccessfully argue for the right to dispose of them themselves, leading to yet another ongoing conflict between the churches), but a few will make their way into the hands of lawmen or resourceful criminals.

The Wild Spirits of Gaff County

The Wild Spirits of Gaff County is intended as a Yarn to follow after The Villains' Bible in a Serial. With some modification it can also be run as a solitary Yarn, though in this case the party should have a past history with Braying Kine as well as with Grover Autumn. However, be warned, this Yarn may significantly change certain parts of the world of Ludt, and so may not be suited to every Judge's vision of the setting; alternatively, should the Judge wish to depend upon the concept presented in The Book of Autumn that this world is a mirror of the true world, a Judge could continue to run games in an unaltered Ludt later, stating that those Yarns are set within the true world.

To introduce this scenario to your players, tell them that it is a year and a half since the events in Chancellor, and the town of Thistlewine has begun to be beset by violent Peruwac raids. This is especially unfortunate for the J.L. Montegue Line, which has recently expanded to Thistlewine.

☙

THE SCENE

The characters are either already in Thistlewine when the raids begin or (more conveniently) arrive roughly three weeks afterwards upon hearing tales of the attacks. Braying Kine is chieftain of the remaining Peruwac, who seem much revived since the events of City Dogs, though he has not been seen since the raids began. A small boom which had been afforded the town by the recent arrival of the J.L. Montegue Line six months ago (reducing travel time from Thistlewine to Darlington down to only a day and a half) has been almost entirely countered by the exodus of fearful townsfolk fleeing the aggressive natives. Those with experience with the Peruwac will note that they are only violent when sufficiently provoked, and this recent bout of attacks runs counter to their nature.

Those few who have gone out attempting to hunt the Peruwac have come back scarred or not at all; this includes a failed raid led by the local sheriff about four days earlier. They tell tales of ghost-camps full of mist where the wigwams are mirages and masked warriors who cannot die assault them from the shadows.

CR

THE CRYPTOLOGIST

If the characters had previously sought out a cryptologist to translate The Book of Autumn this individual will be engaged in this adventure. Upon entering town they will find that the cryptologist moved to Thistlewine six months prior in an attempt to 'escape the hustle of city life.' Should the characters not previously sought the aid of a cryptologist, this individual is the first person they shall meet upon entering town; this is the assumed scenario, and they will henceforth be referred to as Henry Langmelt.

Henry Langmelt is a small, wiry man with thinning hair and delicate wire-rim glasses, yet he carries himself with the assuredness of a man four times his size. He will dismiss the Peruwac attacks, saying that they will pass. He spends most of his time locked away in his house at the edge of town, finishing his most recent project.

This project was delivered to him six months prior by a Peruwac in an elaborate headdress (this is the shaman, Marches with Fear) in the form of a letter. The letter was written in Shuggrak, and a coded message proved the perfect way to gain Henry's interest. It was a letter from Grover Autumn, offering to hire him to translate The Book of Autumn into common parlance. Langmelt accepted and the manuscript arrived in the mail a week later. He has worked fevrishly on the task since, and is nearly finished; the cryptologist even believes that he may have discovered new depths to the manuscript not previously identified by Grover, and has added his own footnotes and appendices.

Should the party confront Langmelt they will find him to be totally mad. He is willing to go to any length to defend his work, and is effectively immortal, with only complete dismemberment halting his assault.

☙

GROVER AUTUMN AND THE NEW EDUCATE CHRONICLE

Investigation into other changes in Thistlewine in the interim will reveal that six months ago (around the same time that Henry Langmelt moved into town and the J.L. Monetgue line established itself) a new printing shop opened up called Misham & Sons. Misham & Sons is only open by appointment (to be made by mail), and their windows are shuttered at all hours. It is operated by a low-ranking member of the Order of Autumn named Harvey Misham. There has been little business for them since opening, and local consensus is that they will soon be out of business. However, in the last few days they have begun working ceaselessly, and their presses can be heard working at all hours.

It requires an inquiry filed with the magistrate's

office in Darlington to determine that Misham & Sons is owned by the Hedermeier Coalition in Chancellor, and a further investigation with the magistrate's office in Chancellor will reveal that the Hedermeier Coalition is owned entirely by Grover Autumn through his controlling interest in the Chancellor Post. All of this will take significant effort and significant time.

At the time of the Yarn, Henry Langmelt has just delivered the final manuscript of his book to the offices of Misham & Sons, which has begun its first print-run of The New Educate Chronicle. The launch of the book will be six months from the start of the Yarn—plenty of time to investigate the ownership of Misham & Sons.

Grover Autumn will arrive in Thistlewine for the release and give a speech while distributing free copies of the occult text to all in attendance. Two weeks before this the printer will ship crates filled with copies of the book to every library, bookstore, and administrative office in the N.L.P. Should all of this be allowed to occur uninterrupted it shall lead to the worst possible ending, discussed later under The Descent.

C3

THE PERUWAC

The Peruwac have indeed returned, in a much more literal sense than could be expected; the only living Peruwac in the area are Braying Kine and his advisor, the mysterious shaman known as Marches with Fear. The warriors leading the violent raids are in fact the spirits of dead Peruwac warriors, masked with the faces of totem animals and manipulated by Marches with Fear's occult influence. Their glassy stares betray no emotion and they make no sound. The masks are markedly different in design from the fox masks from The Villains' Bible, as they are actual ceremonial artifacts for the natives. Their Features should vary, as they did in life, but all rolls against them on Damage Tables should be reduced by 1.

A Match 4 Learnin' roll may identify not only that it is unusual for the Peruwac to wear these masks in war, but also that they represent protective spirits, which often serve as advisors, psychopomps, and occa-

sionally defenders of the village. Active raids on an enemy are not the purview of protector spirits.

Should the characters investigate the Peruwac—a very likely event—they face a harrowing experience. On the way to the old Peruwac village they will be beset on all sides by haunting mists and the ghosts of perceptions. Shadowy figures, armed with bows, axes, and long knives are glimpsed following them or ranging ahead, and even in the light of day the sky is obscured by the otherworldly vapours. The players, not merely their characters, should feel on edge.

As the characters near the village, they will be attacked by six spirits. This will call for Match 4 Bravery rolls. If the characters attempt to communicate with them, they will recognize the spirits of a dead Peruwac which they knew in life (perhaps Triumphant Oak or Crying Pig), though they never remove their mask; this will call for another Bravery roll for the ones who originally succeeded, but this time at Match 6. All such assassins are on foot.

Should the party defeat the spirit-assassins they can easily find their way to the Chief's longhouse. Here they can confront Braying Kine and his advisor.

The Chief is a shadow of his former, proud self, kept docile with powerful opiates by Marches with Fear; if he is addressed directly he will be able to attempt to shake off the spell of the drug, and if he is brought back to the waking world he will stay Marches with Fear and attempt to broker peaceful talks. Appealing to the chieftain's honour is an especially effective way to shake him out of his stupor. He believes himself to be a good ruler who has brought a new golden age to his tribe, and is unaware of the raids or any recent events. In reality, what remained of his village moved on further west and joined with another settlement when they saw the influence that Marches with Fear was having on their once rational and noble ruler. If Marches with Fear is defeated, Braying Kine will return west to the rest of his people and will eventually recover, once more becoming the respected and wise tribal leader he has always been at heart.

Marches with Fear will support everything his master says, while simultaneously hinting at the untrustworthiness of the visitors and praising the Chieftain's rulership. Should the party attack Marches with Fear he will take cover behind Braying Kine's Seat and fire at the party with his ancient fivegun. Every two rounds after the first two new spirits will respond to his call and aid him; these spirits do not trigger new Bravery rolls—this particular horror has already been confronted. Slaying Marches with Fear, knocking him unconscious, or removing or destroying the necklace he wears about his neck will cause the ghosts and the mists to dissipate. Marches with Fear must sleep for eight hours with the pendant on in order to regain its powers; it will not function for anyone else.

MARCHES WITH FEAR

Gumption ··············2

Civilization ···········1

Grit ·················5

Learnin' ·············4

Marches with Fear is not a strong-willed individual. Tired of the lack of purpose in his life which he perceived as being ignored by the spirits he had devoted his life to communing with, he was easily seduced by the Order of Autumn and agreed to protect Thistlewine while the New Educate Chronicle was completed. He knows Grover is the orchestrator of the entire plot, and if captured alive (somehow) he may divulge this information. Additionally, he has a business card on him for Misham & Sons, which lists a registration number; this will greatly speed any inquiry with the Mossbank magistrate's office into the ownership of the printshop. On the back of the card he has written Henry Langmelt's name. He wears a wooden pendant given to him by Grover Autumn in the shape of a fox's head (similar to the fox masks in The Villains' Bible). Marches with Fear in fact never completed his training with his mentor, for his impatience and greed have been present throughout his life. After the confrontation with Marches with Fear, the party will be visited by a party of Peruwac elders led by the defeated's mentor. If he is still alive they will ask that he be surrendered to them; if he is returned to the Peruwac elders he will be punished severely for his heretical hubris. Regardless of whether he lives or not, any characters involved in his defeat will earn a lifelong friendship of the local shamans.

☙

THE DESCENT

Should Grover Autumn be allowed to arrive in town it is likely already too late for Ludt. If the books are shipped out (which, again, will happen two weeks prior to his arrival) the taint of high occultism will have spread across the N.L.P. with little hope of being quelled; someone will one day step in to fill Grover Autumn's boots even should he fail. If Autumn is allowed to give his speech (which may shock those who assumed that his tongue was gone for good), the world will be damned.

As Grover speaks the dark forces at work beneath the skin of Ludt will begin to respond, and a heavy mist will rise, as thick as that which hid the ghostly Peruwac village. By the end of the speech, Thistlewine and Chancellor will have been removed from this domain of existence, becoming their own, new mirror of Ludt which is secretly ruled by Grover Autumn, the two settlements connected by a lonely ghost of the J.L. Montegue Line.

Over time, this mirror domain will begin to create imitations of the surrounding world, until Ludt itself is eventually entirely recreated to service Grover's occult whims. Meanwhile, in reality, Thistlewine and Chancellor will be removed from existence, and only those who have been there within the last few months will remember them, with the rest of the world reshaping itself to accommodate the fact that neither settlement ever existed (a new capital will be found for Pendleton Province, etc.). Anyone in Chancellor or Thistlewine at the time of The Descent will remain in the mirror-dream forever. Only these two settlements are affected, as they are locations closely linked to the machinations of Grover Autumn, and even though he believes he has discovered the heart of Ludt's truth he has only scratched the surface; Ludt will let him have his victory, but will not relinquish the rest of its lands.

Should Grover be slain after he takes the podium in the center of town, but before he finishes the speech, Thistlewine and Chancellor will remain in reality, but they will become hubs for terrifying and unexplainable phenomena, and both will become shunned by many—out of superstition or out of caution.

The only way to entirely save Ludt and the expanding West is to slay Grover before he can deliver his speech and to stop the distribution of books. These are independent of one another, and Grover Autumn can still give his speech should The New Educate Chronicle not go to print.

A City Man

Five hundred federal notes.

Bring him back to Chancellor for five hundred notes, six if alive. Dead or alive, he was coming back to Chancellor.

Ernest Boragne was focused. Utterly focused. As the train rattled along its tracks through the dusty badlands beyond civilization he repeated his quarry's price again and again. Five hundred notes, six if alive.

There was another passenger in the car. A fat old fellow with a bowler cap and a frayed suit. He had fallen asleep with the latest issue of the Chancellor Post across his face, and the thin pages fluttered as he snored. The passenger had already been asleep when Boragne boarded, and he had no intention of waking him. The dust on his shins made clear that he was one of the fools hoping to make a fortune in the west. Boragne knew how good it was to live in the city where it was clean and you didn't have to break the law just to get by – he had never felt the urge to leave it behind for fantasies of new frontiers.

Boragne was gaunt and his black hair, slicked back into a sharp peak, had begun to whiten at the roots. He bore a few days' shadow on his cheeks and was dressed in a crisp grey suit, complete with new bow tie and long jacket. His bowler cap sat on his lap with his fingers laced over it as his brown eyes stared at the sleeping figure and through him, unfocused on the world. Focused only on his thoughts.

Five hundred federal notes.

She had said it wasn't enough. Six if alive, he had reminded her. But it wasn't enough. She said he should be done with this life. But where would she be without his money? Where would she be if he didn't take these contracts?

The train rattled and creaked as it pulled into another dead-end stop. Out here the towns were little more than the stations themselves. No brick buildings. No industry. No culture. Just wooden fronts behind which were bars and bordellos and bally poor moneylenders. The frontier was for dreamers and the doomed. Boragne reached into his pocket and checked the time. His watch was silver and embossed with small flowers. She had given it to him for his fortieth birthday, just after his father had died.

With a snort the paper slid off the other passengers' face as he sat up, listening to the whistle blow. He rubbed his piggy eyes and brushed out his thick grey mustache. He looked to be older than Boragne by at least ten years.

"My apologies. I suppose I was a tad more tired than I assumed. I didn't notice you board. I'm er... Name's Todd. Benjamin Todd."

"Pleasure to meet you, Mr. Todd." But Boragne did not look at all pleased. "I am Ernest Boragne. I boarded at St. Amon. I transferred from the J. L. Montegue line out of Chancellor."

"A Chancellor man? My, my. We don't get many city boys out this far West. What line of work're you in? Me, I'm in investments."

Investments. Most likely he was in land, selling dry plots to prospectors with promises of silver and gold. Boragne was not a boy, nor did he like the sound of this man's palaver. "I'm with the Acquisitions Union." He looked out the window, willing Mr. Todd to cease his prattling.

"A Functional? Well, isn't that exciting!" He leaned forward, but only so far, since his great gut quickly got in the way, straining the buttons of his cream-coloured shirt. "Tell me, you hunting some great villain? Some fugitive fled from the pen? Anyone I know? Was it in the papers?"

Boragne was done answering the investments man. Aye, he was a Functional as the common folk called him, though she didn't like it. Pursuing wanted men across provincial boundaries where the federal marshals could not go. Each contract paying his way to the next.

Five hundred federal notes, six if alive.

She was worried about his health. Five men in his family dead by fifty of Rugor's Dementia. What few years he had left he should spend at home. He was fine, he had told her. Always told her. The last time she had said it he had hit her so hard she cut her lip on the counter before he left for the station.

He had forgotten his contract and the neighbor had caught him just in time.

But he hadn't forgotten his gun.

☙

He had heard that it got cold at night out in the desert, but by the days you wouldn't know it. He was glad to leave Mr. Todd when he disembarked at Gilestown, but he had feigned regret. It was important to be polite. He scowled as he noted the dust already forming on the ends of his coat. Boragne had no bag and so left the train to find the local constable. As he walked the bare, unpaved street he thumbed at the small writing pad he kept. His leather gloves shielded him from the filth. This was the last place where there had been word of his quarry, sent by a federal auditor named Wiles who remembered the villain's face from the _Post_. The Functional had to work quickly if he wanted to net the payment before a public bounty was posted.

How much would they offer? Two hundred? Three? Certainly not five, six if alive.

A low roof, crooked and buckling, topped the jailhouse. Silhouetted by the afternoon sun, a lone vulture cawed from the rooftop. A wizened old man in an impractically wide-brimmed hat sat in a rocking chair beside the door. His skin was as grey as the uniform he wore, and a tarnished brass star was pinned to his breast.

Boragne stepped forward and tipped the brim of his own cap. He introduced himself and held out his contract, which the man squinted briefly at before dismissing it. "You are the constable, are you not?"

Nodding, he answered, "Name's Ames."

The Functional told the lawman the name of his quarry. Ames said he had seen him when he came through town, but he had caused no trouble. Boragne tipped his hat and thanked the constable, turning to leave, but turned back and asked in what direction the man had traveled.

"I just told ye he took a coach toward Millings. 'Bout four days ago." Constable Ames eyed the visitor strangely and spit. Boragne scowled and went on to hire a horse. It cost him thirty federal notes.

&#x08;

The last contractor had followed the quarry to Vincent's Wake, on the edge of Pendleton Province, where the criminal had killed two farmers. He hadn't had time to do to them what he did in Denbridge or Lossen. Or what he had done in that northern Chancellor burg.

Horrible.

Five hundred federal notes worth of horrible, six if alive.

The horse he'd hired was sturdy and spotted. The stableman said its name was Nod. A local guide had offered to accompany him for five notes, and he had given him three. Three notes was enough money for the Dovanri wanderer.

But five hundred wasn't enough for her, six if alive.

Valio – that was the guide – said that Millings was only two hours' ride from Gilestown, or four by road, since the road followed the cliffs. They would take the shorter ride, to beat the bounty. To save time. She didn't think he had much left.

They set out across dry bluffs between Gilestown and Millings, the rocky ground and Nod's gait doing no favours to Boragne's rear. He did not even remember how long he had been in the business, but he had never taken a liking to horses. He would much rather chase his quarry through cobbled streets than in the dry open air of the counties, but five hundred notes was nothing to scoff at. Unless you were her.

He had loved her once. Hadn't he? She must have looked so beautiful in her youth. But now she was old like him. Her skin had begun to sag and her hair had lost its luster. She worried too much, ragging and moaning about the cost of the doctor one moment and begging him to retire the next. She didn't understand. If he wasn't there to catch degenerates like this, who would? And if he wasn't there to collect the five hundred federal notes, six if alive, who would?

They did not ride hard, for the sun was still high and they were saving time by avoiding the road. Valio, his scarf bright about his neck despite the dust that coated him, offered some dried meat and pickled greens, but they were spiced and Boragne knew after one bite that they would upset his aging gut — he was nearly as old as his father had been when he died. He would eat after Millings. The Dovanri spoke for much of the ride, telling stories and watching the clouds. The Functional did not care for Valio's anecdotes of ghosts and friend- ly thieves, but he remained largely silent.

Entering Millings, Boragne growled low in his throat. If he had not seen the sign outside of town he may have mistaken it for the town they had just left. The same cheap flaky-painted boards and flat roofs greeted him, and the same wan faces, dried out by the sun. The same bally bordello and the same bally general store. His toes curled at the thought of the dreary lives the men and women of this town must lead. Nothing to do but stare at the dust and muse about when they were going to strike big.

They tied their horses before the tavern where, through the batwing doors creaking slightly in the wind, could be seen an empty common room save for one lone drunk and a sad piano player. The untuned piano played the same old song every piano played out here in the west, much too jaunty for the dreary de- serts and sandy bluffs and full of wrong notes and clanging keys. The guide went to join the drunk, hand already gripping the notes just given him, and Boragne left him to find the constable.

Opening his pad again he scanned his written notes from

the last lawman, but he was distracted by the heat and had to stop and read them again. Two times he read them before his eyes focused and his mind settled. She would have panicked and told him it was the Dementia, but it was only the sun.

Constable Myers was younger and talked more than Constable Ames, but the roof of the jail still needed work, and there were still a few crows hanging about, just like before. This time the lawman took the contract and read it thoroughly, being certain of the crimes contained.

"Horrible," he muttered.

"Horrible," Boragne agreed.

Myers asked what the man looked like, and when Boragne described him the lawman swore – the uncultured dog. There was no need for that type of talk. The man had come and bought supplies at the store in town. Supplies for cooking and camping and prospecting. Prospecting wasn't good around Millings, but he wouldn't listen, so they had pointed him in the direction of the small mine north of town, abandoned two years previous by the Mint & Denning Mining Company. There were families up there. Women and children of other hopefuls who refused to believe the mine wasn't worth the effort.

"Help them," begged the constable.

"Aye, no harm will come to them if I can help it."

Before he could leave the man stopped him with a hand on his arm. The hand was layered in dust. "Have you ever seen a heat storm, Mr. Boragne? Oh, well be careful then. We get them around this time of year, 'specially up in them hills. Lightning struck one of the miner's hutches last year. Burned all night. Damn hot too. Fierce as a spooked nag and strange as Hell."

"Mind your tongue around me, Constable."

He could bear this awful place for five hundred notes, but he would not be party to profanity. She was good about that. She never swore, even when he forgot to come home at night.

☙

Valio did not want to go further without more notes, and he would not allow himself to be underbid again. Three more notes to travel to the M&D mine. The drunk had been called Isaac and the pianist Boris.

"It's too rocky for the horses, Mr. Boragne. I know these hills. We must walk, so sorry."

It was not so far to the mine, and Boragne angrily regretted paying Valio for work he could have done himself; a rusted iron scaffold was visible above the hills from just outside of town, and they merely followed it until the sun began to set. The mine at first looked to be set within some low hills, but as the two crested these the Functional saw that M&D had built a pit mine here. So much money wasted on land dry of minerals. Camps were visible dotting the floor of the mine, even in the setting sun. Some featured cheap shacks and careful work-stations to siphon the loam. Others featured a tent and a sieve, and sometimes just a bedroll with a shovel and a waterjug. On the far side was a black mark where Valio said the lightning had struck as Constable Myers had said, but a new hovel was already built over the ruins of the old. If life in Millings and Gilestown was sparse, this life was as near to true misery as Boragne had yet seen. He mumbled a prayer to Saint Lorraine for steadfastness in his quest and absently thumbed the hilt of his sixgun, bright and unblemished inside his long coat. The chamber under the hammer was empty to avoid accident. His suit was ruined and it had been barely a day. Filthy and wind-scarred. But he could buy a new one once he was paid.

Stumbling down the rocky side of the mine, they

eventually found solid footing near the edge of a grey-ing hut which sloped dangerously to one side. Valio had wrapped his bright scarf around his face and so was not beset by the same fit of coughing that betook his em-ployer. The door to the hovel slammed loudly open on the other side and a balding man with a white beard came cautiously around the corner, long gun in hand.

"Who're you? What're you doin' 'ere? This's my claim. Get yer city boots off my tract. Oy! Dovy! Hands where I can see 'em!"

But Boragne's contract was enough to assuage the man's fears, though he still would not lower his weapon from the guide.

He and his brothers manned this plot – two whole acres – and had since the mine closed. They had been em-ployed there, but now the Nolan brothers were operating on their own. They had made twenty-three notes selling gold in those two years, but they knew a big break was coming; no-one else had found anything yet, which meant their plot had the greatest chance of scoring. At least according to them.

Boragne was once more glad of the few hundred notes he would make, more if his quarry lived.

Herb, the Nolan who had greeted them with his ri-fle, told them that his brothers were sleeping. He would not have invited them in, "in any case," he assured them, just so they were clear where they stood with him. He knew the man they sought and had seen him working an-other plot.

"Those damned Emersons down on the east side."

"Watch your language, Mr. Nolan."

Herb Nolan made a face and spit.

Traveling to the eastern side they had easily found the Emerson plot. Not one, but two shacks stood

here, both sturdier than the Nolans' and freshly painted
in a bright shade of blue. As the light died men were
leaving their sieves and shovels and brushes and picks
where they lay and gathering about a fire. A few brief
questions confirmed that the Emersons hired plenty of
labour - they were rich and barely visited the site
themselves.

"But isn't the gold gone?" asked Valio.

"We ain't diggin' gold 'ere," answered
Mitch, one of the workers, his face
stained, "We're mining coal. Some o'
the other plots 'ave caught on as
well."

"Is there a Mr. Emerson here?"

"No sir, Mr. Functional,
sir."

He asked them if they knew a
man who matched the description in his contract, and
they all nodded aye. He could see by their eyes that he
was not well liked. Unsurprising, for a man so soulless
so as to do such awful things to his own family. And the
victims in Denbridge and Lossen, to say nothing of the
farmers he had slain near Vincent's Wake.

She had wanted a family. Or he had. It all got
muddled after she started worrying over his health. He
forgot so many things in his anger with her. Why would-
n't she believe him when he told her he wasn't losing
his mind? There was no mania to dull his senses. No
fugue to prevent him earning a few hundred notes, more
if he did well.

They asked if the man had a bounty yet and eyed
him evilly when he told them no. Boragne resolved then
to hurry in case they disbelieved him and made to apprehend or kill his prey before he could find him. The
quarry had beaten a man named Jules yesterday morning

and been forced out by the foreman. Foreman Walsh said he thought he'd seen the fugitive working with some small camp on the north lip, but he wasn't certain.

"I knew there wasn't no good in that man."

"Why didn't you go to Constable Myers?" But the look Walsh gave him told him that to them Myers was of the same world as Boragne, and that world and theirs did not mix.

At least they were agreed.

It was very warm and the labourers mused that a storm might be coming.

"The heat will drop with sunset, and then it'll pick right back up and burn like whistlin'."

"There's no protection if the lightning comes for you," chirped Valio.

"None save prayer."

Boragne nodded at the man who had spoken. Prayer was always safe, even if you didn't remember all of the words.

As they walked to the lip of the mine Valio chewed absently on his rations. All the men here were grimy and caked in dirt, and what few women and children he saw seemed even worse. None of them appeared to have ever bathed and their breaths all stank of alcohol. Boragne did not drink. He used to, but the doctor had told him that he needed to quit. At least that was what she said, but he couldn't clearly remember what the doctor had said to him. She worried when he said that. But no one listens to doctors. Not closely.

"Why are you still with me, Mr. Valio? You're job is done and I am paying you no more."

"I'll leave soon enough, Mr. Boragne, but I don't intend to head back tonight and I would appreciate the chance to see a Functional arrest such a vile criminal. You did not tell me before how deplorable his deeds were."

An arrest. Or a gunfight. It was a few hundred federal notes one way, and more the other. Either way it was good money.

At the northern ridge they found a half dozen camps, but the first they came to was empty. The coals of the fire were cold, and in the dusk Boragne could not see a trail. He led Valio to the next tent, luckily finding the man awake, but he had not seen those campers for much of the day. They visited another plot and a jolly man named Lon said he didn't know them. At the following camp the man looked confused and said he had not seen them for much of the day.

Valio eyed his employer strangely. "Do you not remember Benny, Mr. Boragne? It can't have been ten minutes."

Of course he remembered Benny, he had merely needed to make certain. One can never be too careful when such a violent man is concerned. In Denbridge their intestines had been entirely removed and their ribs splayed so the heart and lungs could be taken. At Lossen all that was left were the bones and the blood. Sometimes Boragne thought she was as frightened by the things he must see, the people he must catch, as by the imagined dementia she cried over and berated him about. He had never felt an inclination to be violent with her before her paranoia about his health.

Finally they visited a tent where a man named Casper told them through his muskrat whiskers that they had left for the deeper hills with their new hired hand around noon. He had expected them back, for they had left their tent. There were two of them – a father and

son both named John. Casper pointed them toward a blu-
ish plateau some ways distant. There was supposed to be
silver there, but the natives talked of spirits, so he
had never gone. These country folk were superstitious
and foolish. But he thanked the prospector and let him
return to his beans, which he had offered and been de-
nied. Boragne's stomach rumbled. He had forgotten to eat
in town. But beans in brown sugar was not a decent meal
and he had no intention of facing his quarry with the up
-set a meal of beans would cause him. He would eat later
that night. Or tomorrow.

଼

More walking. His boots were sturdy, but they were
scuffed now. They were not the garish high boots the men
wore out west here, but sensible boots. Boots you should
pay to have shined. His spurs jangled in the dust. He
hated spurs, but he had known he may be riding and the
horses in these parts were likely to be green. The horses would have been useful now.

Valio had returned to his talk of ghosts and des-
peradoes and promiscuous farmers' wives. Nonsense. But
it was better than the silence of the desert. Barely.
Boragne walked in silence as the sun set and the temper-
ature fell.

One tale did manage to catch his attention however, and he asked the Dovanri to begin it again. The wanderer's dark eyes lit up and he began once more. Telling
of the Wendigo and its hunger for flesh. A spirit walking in the form of a man, but the man would not know
those he loved and they would not know him. Like a wild
dog it would begin with those for whom its heart had
once beat strongest, and with each life it took it would
become less human and more predator. Hunting and killing. Killing and eating. Eating and eating. Eating until
there was nothing left of it but the haunt within the
man and it could stand no longer in the world. But the

Wendigoag could stay in this world for centuries before their tastes pulled them else.

Boragne shuddered despite himself. Shuddered at the cold.

"Where did you hear of this, Mr. Valio?"

"From a Peruwac hunter in Gaff County. He said that his uncle had become Wendigo and slain their entire village. He had only survived, Mr. Boragne, by reasoning with the last of the humanity in the Wendigo. He offered to show me the site of his village, but I declined. I have never met a Peruwac hunting alone before or since." His eyes were still bright with the tale, but he looked strangely frightened as well. "His face was long and grey, and his nose flat. He was young, but his cheeks hung low and his ears were long on the top. Never have I seen so strange a man, Mr. Boragne."

"Many Peruwac are ugly." The childish fear Boragne had felt was gone. "It was a good legend, but the theatrics at the end weakened the telling. Next time leave them off, Mr. Valio."

He was glad that Valio did not voice the same thought that had come to him at the telling of the story. Had Valio chosen that myth on purpose?

It was cold but Borgane had worn layers. His hand sat restlessly on his sixgun as they neared the earthen monolith.

છ

Towering into the young night sky, the wall of the plateau was not as sheer as it looked from afar, and craggy paths spiraled up its sides. Not as sheer, but taller still than it had ever looked from afar. It was hot. Had it been so hot on the walk from the pit?

Boragne stopped to gaze dumbly at the stars twinkling dimly in the inky blue sky. Something rumbled in the distance. That sky and those stars. If those could be seen in Chancellor he perhaps would spend more time out at night. Nights spent out on purpose. Not wandering because he had not thought to go home. Would she still worry then? Of course she would. She was paranoid. So paranoid she could not even see how good it would be to be paid the notes for this contract.

Dead or alive, some hundred credits in his hands.

"Mr. Boragne," the Dovanri called. By the starlight Boragne could make out a dark stain, which Valio was touching gingerly. They should have brought a lantern, but it had not occurred to them as they left. "Had we brought a lantern as I suggested we could see more clearly, so sorry to bring it up again, but I think this is blood. It is cold and dry, but the sun has not yet bleached it away." The Functional did not need to be told that it was blood, nor that it was from today. He glared at the back of the Dovanri's soft cap. Valio turned his head to meet his eye. "I am not a fighter, Mr. Boragne, and I do not wish to die. I will wait for you here."

"You come all this way just to leave now?" Boragne was incensed, despite the usual lonely manner of his profession.

The guide shrank back, his hands raised. "I do not wish to die, so sorry. I will wait here and call for you if there is danger. Call like an owl. I know many sounds, Mr. Boragne."

Red-faced and sputtering, the Functional looked up past the brim of his cap at the stony tower above him. "Do you at least have a gun to defend yourself?"

"No, Mr. Boragne, only my knife."

ભ

Bats flapped about the path as Boragne struggled

up it alone. He must have knocked a stone loose or made some terrible sound to disturb them so. That would make it much harder to surprise his prey. One of the foul things had even shit on his new coat. It was ruined now. But he would buy a new one with the bounty. It was so hot, but he refused to remove his coat. He didn't want to lose it.

Why didn't she want the money?

He took care of her, and he made good money hunting fugitives. She was ungrateful. She didn't care. This was his life. When he returned home he would tell her how things would be. She wouldn't berate him for his choices. She wouldn't complain about his late nights or when he was absent-minded because his work had been tiring. It was for her, and she didn't understand.

A few hundred credits to kill a cannibal.

He could do that.

Halfway up the slope he found two canvas shoulder bags and a pile of tools. Sieves and shovels and brushes and picks. The bags were stained black. Blood. He had thought he would find blood. He had known it, somehow. The blood trailed up the path, toward the summit. Drawing his sixgun, he spun the cylinder so the empty chamber was no longer under the hammer. There was no moon, but the stars glinted silver off his holy arm, and he muttered a half-remembered prayer as he began stalking up the path.

Along the sides of the cliff were old native draw-
ings. He passed a trio of old huts built into the hill,
made of dark stone or clay. Lines and swirls and incom-
prehensible scribblings - his eyes came unfocused when
he looked upon them. But he was not here to look at history. Sweat beaded on his brow. He stopped and angrily
scrubbed at the stone with his sleeve, but the writing
would not be undone. Somewhere a coyote howled and he
barked back at it, wordlessly.

Thunder shook the sky and a flash of lightning
followed swiftly after. Stepping back, he blinked and
looked at the wall, then down at his frayed jacket. It
was ruined. He would have to find a way to pay for a new
one. But now he had to kill the cannibal.

Weapon in hand and shoulders hunched, he resumed
his cautious stalk up the hillside, his spurs rattling
like snakes with each step. Closer and closer. Thunder
rumbling. Lightning burning the distant dust. Closer.
Soon he could see the crest, the starlight and the
lightning ricocheting off it so it seemed to glow and
flash in the dimness. As he neared the top he could hear
a noise. A humming. Or a whistling. Some small noise
among the crashing of the storm.

"I'm coming home, Helen."

The top of the plateau was smooth and black, dark-
er than the stony paths below. Tall stones stood or lay
scattered about and the stars were mirrored in them
darkly. The heat trapped itself in the stones and filled
the peak with choking warmth. The humming was greater
here and he cautiously set one food forward, afraid for
a moment he would somehow trip and fall into Hell. But
his boot met dark sand and he continued on. The storm
split the sky and rumbled like deep laughter. He looked
about, watching for movement. A part of him sang out to
look back, for he could surely see the lights of his

home from here. But he must be vigilant.

He nearly fell over the corpse. Looking down, he paused. His gaze lingered for a long moment at the face of the boy illuminated in the crashing lightning, his dead jaw frozen open in fear. Did he know this boy? Where would they have met? The boy's stomach was open, and his ribs cracked. His in-
sides were gone – no-
where to be seen – and bestial toothmarks were visible along his arms and near his groin. Black blood pooled thickly in his open throat and the cavi-
ty of his chest. Boragne began to hum along to the unearthly tune.

He called the cannibal's name and fired off a shot at a fleeting shadow, then two more as he spun, unsure. Bats flew up in clouds then, spiraled back to their routines. The coyote howled and Boragne barked back.

Pacing between the stones, he soon found another staring death in the storm. This man was much the same as the boy, but his fingers too were gnawed and his wound reached deep between his thighs, empty. Boragne wondered if lightning could do such damage. He stood above the corpse and stared at it and through it, unfocused on the world. Focused only on his thoughts. What had he forgotten? He hummed to help himself remember. Why was he here? Where was here? He felt his fingers loosening on his sixgun as he realized the humming had stopped and he gripped it tightly, spinning and firing again.

The bullet skimmed one of the black rocks near to his face as the storm crackled and dust flew into his eyes. The Functional cried out and swore, pawing at his face, his gun still gripped firmly in one gloved hand. His eyes ached with the rock dust and stung at his eyelids. The gloves he wore were too bulky and he threw them to the ground, gasping as he blinked in agony.

There was a shape above him and it offered him water. Thankfully, he rinsed his eyes with the canteen, blinking until he could see. See the cannibal before him. He raised his gun, but the fugitive lifted a blackened hand and warned him, "You don't know what else is out here. Shhh..."

He lowered his weapon and nodded. He did not want to attract anything dangerous. He was from the city and did not know what dangers this mesa could hold. The man looked different than the photograph he had seen in Chancellor. It had been an old photo. People change. This man had less hair, and it hung in straggling strands. He had jowls and a flat nose and his ears drooped, almost to points. And his teeth. Long teeth with small gums. Sharp teeth. Sunken eyes. And he hummed. That was the humming. It was the man with the water.

"I am supposed to find you. My name is Ernest Boragne."

"Aye, that seems right." He eyed Boragne and his black orbs reflected red in the lightning. "Tell me, Mr. Boragne, are you ill?"

Boragne nodded. What was he doing here? "I think I'm dying."

"That is too bad, Mr. Boragne. Come, sit." He followed the man to a small fire and sat beside it. He loosened his collar and slid out of his jacket, dripping with sweat. A rich smell came from a skillet resting on the coals. It seemed hot enough to cook without a fire. "What are you dying of?" His voice was low and guttural, but he spoke so well. Like a city man.

"Rugor's Dementia." That was right, wasn't it? "I forget things." He took the plate he was offered gratefully. He did not remember the last time he had eaten.

"What sorts of things?"

He could feel the slow tears on his face, cold in the heat. What didn't he remember? His gun was still firmly in his grip and his finger twitched on the trigger, the metal burning on his skin. "Everything."

"Do you want a fork, Mr. Boragne?" He nodded and thanked his friend as one was set on his plate. Friend? No, he didn't know this man.

"You don't have to die, Mr. Boragne."

"I don't?" He could not grab the fork because he was holding his sixgun. It glittered in the starlight, then flashed in the lightning.

"No." The man was eating and drooling, his long face canine in the ghoulish flickering of the flames. "All you have to do is eat."

Boragne's mouth watered as he looked upon the meat, pooling in ripe juice, and his finger twitched on the trigger.

A Thank You to My Patrons

Brady Murphy, Malilda, S.Rintoul, Kate Jennings, Luke Murphy, and Terra Jansma.

It is by your support that I am able to keep producing. Thank you.

About the Author

F. Killian lives with his dog Howard in an old parsonage in a small midwestern town. A lifetime of interest in myth, fantasy, and rumour has bred in him a healthy fascination with the spiritual, historical, and occult. When he is not rolling dice at the tabletop or drawing, he is walking in the expansive forests and hills near his home and writing fiction or keeping company with the various goblins, ghouls, and gnomes which follow him wherever he goes.